through the lane

to St. Anne ...

Three

E. Sandy Powell

One World Learning Company

Published in the United States of America

Library of Congress Control Number: 2017906662
ISBN: 978-0-9859088-7-4

First Edition: May 2017

The St. Anne series is a work of fiction.
For more of Powell's writing and dance:
www.esandypowell.com

This book's for you, Pop.
Your patient, while eager, waiting for each new book
has meant so much to me.

♥

Through the lane to St. Anne ...

Lorena started it.

"Mare! Hooray! You're ..."

But she was gone, around the corner, then in seconds "... back!" shoving the toaster into Mare's hands.

"All right, Lorena, I'll get to it. Soon as I can."

"Good then. This bonky bonk," thumping it, "toaster! Works for everybody, but not for me! Since you left, hardly ever a good pop tart ..."

"Hey! This can't be the place I left then. Since when do we have pop tarts at St. Anne?"

"We got to eat a lot of ..." Lorena halfway turned. Eyes blanked, though her body was pointing in the direction her mind had gone. End of hall. La cuisine. Mouth opened ... Closed. There was no way Lorena could catch Mare up on Thom and Regoire's trip.

Lorena drifted further, in … to their own gentle people, Lorena's and Chet's, and Aggie's of course. Aggie … So much had transpired while Mare was away. Naturally Lorena snagged, no wonder she trailed off.

"And what's this!"

Snap. Back in her body, Lorena's arm shot out, protective cup to her hand. "Who. It's a who."

And there was Aggie, toddling from the kitchen to her momma.

Mare dropped in a squat, "So this is the Aggie-who Delaney told me about, and wow, Who is growing so fast. You were just a baby when I saw you last."

"Aggie." Lorena fingered the shoulders wobbling up alongside her, while she placed her outstretched palm over Aggie's ear. "Mare, you don't have to talk to Aggie in rhymes."

Pretend peering around behind Aggie, "I only see one of

you, but I'll bet you're entwined all through St. Anne's." Mare motioned loops around herself rather than pressing into Aggie's space. "Yeah, I'll bet you inspire more pretzelized odes than anything as confined as a rhyming couplet, don't you." Mare brought her contortioning to a close with the toss of an imaginary ball up high in the air.

Intercepting the lob, Chet stepped in, or rather lunged in from a crawl, as he'd been on hands-and-knees duty in the kitchen and hadn't pulled out of it yet, while Lorena fumbled, "I don't know what you're talking about."

"Never mind me, Lorena, I'm being goofy. Hey Chet."

"Hi Mare." He placed a bobbing hand at Aggie's back, which Aggie liked, as long as Chet let up before he jostled her off balance.

Chet kept lined up, straight as he could, backing his little family, taking it upon himself to intercede if he thought Lorena or Aggie needed help. Lorena had worked hard enough to get Celeste to see their child as who she was at any given moment, not who others imagined, nor who she might some day become.

Chet reached, about to pick up his daughter, but broke off mid move. He often changed courses in his fatherly maneuvering as he picked up on Lorena's wants. Chet leaned back, back against the wall, let Aggie be, clamped to her momma.

Aggie dimpled. For no apparent reason. Aggie does.

"Aggie's not the only … different at St. Anne. We'll ask Mulch about your workbench, won't we Chet. We can put it back together wherever you want."

"caawwah."

"caawwah?" Mare tried to look serious, eyebrow cocked, but could not help an out-of-character twinkle.

Aggie dimpled back, reason apparent.

"Mulchy won't mind moving his tools, will he Chet."

4

Lorena fiddled Aggie's topknot. Her daughter had that arm of hers, the one that had refused to grow, locked tight around Lorena's knee. "Your daddy will straighten things out, won't you Chet."

"We've been missing a vise, Mare."

"Well don't look at me!" but neither picked up on either entendre.

Celeste, though, did smile inside. Seated several yards away, Celeste was doing well at keeping herself in check. You know the feeling 'so drenched in endearment' that you dare not put your emotion into action, heaven forbid into words, not within earshot lest you scare beloveds off? Celeste held to from the gathering room with a quiet "Hello, Mare."

Mare, kneeling now in front of Aggie, allowed her cheeks to relax just short of a smile too as she tipped a light nod in Celeste's direction while holding focus on Aggie.

"sh-lls-shshh" the squeak pipped.

5

"sh-llls-shshhsh" Mare mouthed back.

Celeste noted. And no offense taken.

"Celeste," Lorena enthused, "we were just working out where we can fit in Mare's work bench. She's got this toaster to fix. Did you know she was coming? I could have bought pop tarts."

"And metal snips. Mare's going to need new metal snips. We've been using your old ones for cutting the corn stalks, and ..."

"... limb trimm'n," Lorena extended.

"Mulch didn't think ..."

"Mulch always thinks, Chet. He just thought Mare wasn't coming back."

Chet nodded, excusing everyone with his shoulder hops. "We'll get you some new ones, won't we Aggie."

Aggie took a step towards Mare, "ahgr"

A smile actually parted Mare's pursed lips, "ahgr"

6

"ʳbbrhr"

"Mmm, I'm glad."

"Do you speak her language? Celeste, Mare speaks Aggie's language!"

Celeste held her watchful body tone. A direct overture and Mare might flee. Or at least that's how fragile ... no, precious, Mare's return palpated inside Celeste.

"ʳbbuhbbarrr"

"ʳbbuhbbarrr too"

"Regoire!" Lorena couldn't contain herself.

Regoire stuck his head out la cuisine door. Even from down the hall he took in Lorena's fever. And Chet's undergirding, Mare's cool, and ... 'Where was Celeste, was she holding her tongue?' Regoire would have been concerned, but she didn't seem to be hovering so he pieced together Celeste must be out of his sight line, within but on the periphery of Mare's return.

"Mare! Welcome. Lorena can you tell me in one minute? I've got two rows of ..." winking "coming out of the oven." And without adding details, Regoire ducked back to his work, but immediately poked his head out again, "Tea in just a bit, Mare. We'll see you then, yes?"

From la cuisine, Regoire dialed Thom, not knowing if he'd be caught up in mediation, wanting to give him the chance to pop over though if he could. Regoire had to hold for voice messaging ...

"I'm going to get Mulch. Are you coming Lorena?"

Lorena followed Chet out through the gathering room, scooping Aggie up as she went. At the door to the garden, Lorena passed Aggie to Chet.

"wshoo"

"wshoo" Mare bid Aggie off.

Celeste wheeled into the entry, indicated the front door, "Walk with me?" then called down the hall. "Ten minutes, Regoire?"

Regoire fluttered his hand out into the hall, 'yes yes,' then flashed five fingers three times as he had the hand-held tucked at his ear, a tart tin clutched in his other hand. Waving a 'Wait' though, Regoire set the tin around on a counter, juggled the phone and called, "Half an hour" pinching his fingers, "maybe a bit more."

The nearly reunited let him know that they'd heard. Mare held the door so Celeste could wheel through.

Chapter 2 ~ Repaired

fr Middle French
reparer

"Dear, it's good to see you."

"Celeste ..."

"If we must, at some point, we can discuss at length. Today would it be all right with you to simply look forward? I'm eager to hear what you've been thinking and dreaming."

Mare laughed. The rough edge to her jaw was unchanged, her hair more unruly than ever. What might spring forth at any next minute, one couldn't be sure when it came to Mare. Celeste wasn't surprised by Mare's tenderness toward Aggie. What did flummox Celeste from time to time over the years was Mare's coming off as crude in certain situations. So how did one account for their connection? As different as they were, there was no denying something between them, well beyond their pairing up at the drums.

"Lorena always did go straight to the point, didn't she. Bringing out that broken toaster the minute she saw me! Would you say Lorena's psychic, Celeste?"

"Does it matter?"

To Mare it didn't matter in the least. Shooting straight arrow herself, unless, that is, she sometimes grabbed a bent one from her quiver, or found her aim impossibly botched when drawn to another equally fractured soul.

Mare took a breath. Checking in with herself it seemed nearly okay to open up.

"Lorena called it, Celeste. I expect hers is not the only broken toaster in town. I'm going to set up a shop ... or as soon as I can I'm going to. Mulch might know of a good location. Empty building somewhere. I searched for competition online. Delaney backed me up. Neither of us could find a small appliance repair, or anything along the lines of a fix-it service up or down the coast. For sure none in town. There was that guy over by the Slurp 'n Toot but he's been gone, long time now."

Celeste had learned. Keep the praise to a minimum. Give Mare breathing room. Celeste didn't say a thing … not at first.

But she did turn them towards the pathway that led in the direction of … then thought better of it. The last time she and Mare had been down that path, she'd soon had to send Mare's extempore friend, Love, and his marimba troop packing, off the property. And Mare had gone with.

"Let's take the long way round. You don't mind do you?"

But Mare did. She stepped in front of Celeste's wheel-chair, then backed up and sat herself on the near end of the stone wall. Celeste was obliged to roll towards her if the conversation was to continue.

"Celeste I'm going to apologize, then okay we'll be done. I can't imagine. It must have made no sense to you. I guess I had to … What followed wasn't all bad except for the way it wedged you and I apart. 'Unconscionable,' I kept telling myself, but I didn't know how to make it right. I am so sorry for taking the … for taking your marimba."

12

Mare's voice dropped into husky as she strained to pull it back from a crack. "That was ... me at my worst. Really poor judgment in the heat of some strong emotions. I hope you can trust me enough, maybe down the road, so I can still visit you all at St. Anne."

"Heavens, Mare, of course you can, and not in some future. We all do things that later we realize we could've done bet ... differently. You returned the marimba. I appreciated that. Just now you've completed what amends you wanted to make. We're settled."

Mare eyed Celeste. What was the point of dragging this out? She'd been prepared for it taking a long time, for what she'd done being a big deal. Now that it wasn't, Mare needed a second to catch up. But only a second. She let out her laugh.

"Were you wanting to walk, Celeste?" Celeste's satisfied smile could be maddening but Mare knew how this went. She shook off perturbation by playing around the edges of intractableness herself, "What's with this wheelchair,

13

Celeste? Can you get up out of there!" Mare presented her arm and Celeste took it, attempting to turn them out the lane but Mare still wouldn't have it.

"We're going forward from here, just as you said Celeste. I happen to like this path." And she set them on it, walking in low gear, Celeste at her elbow.

They said nothing more as they passed through the stone walls at either side, past the cleaning cubby, on round the loop past the reflective pool and over the arched bridge. From there the path hadn't been tended quite as well. Celeste wondered if she might mention to Mulch, but he and 'the kids' had been going full bore with the vegetable garden. She decided to let him get to it on his own. The way Mulch worked, she knew he would.

"I haven't been out here in such a long time."

Celeste patted at the undergrowth as they made their way kitty-corner, heading across the entire lot. Well past the place where the marimba troop had parked their big rig, Celeste smiled at stalks grown back, leaves filled out

14

on that swipe 'Love's bus' had made on the Oregon grapes. Beyond that clearing though, the path became choked, Nootka rose in the last sunny spot, further on thick salal and rhododendron. Celeste had slowed almost to a stop anyway.

"I've been thinking," she mused off-handedly, which didn't in the least fool Mare. "Delaney told me you might be returning, and she did happen to mention your shop plans ... I hope you don't mind."

Mare's smile puckered in the left corner. Celeste hadn't remembered that expression. Something newly acquired perhaps.

Celeste gave a flick of her index finger as if scouring out the shrubbery. "The boulevard is really close."

Mare pointed too. "Is that what you're ..." But Mare stopped, looked to Celeste.

Celeste couldn't meet her gaze but she did tiptoe toward answering, "You remember when I sold my Z24."

"Oo! That was one of the few cars I got to work lead on. What a beauty. Smooth tune-ups."

"I'm forever grateful to Sadie for making me aware of your talents." Celeste squeezed Mare's hand but immediately adjusted as Mare involuntarily pulled back. Celeste hurried on, "Right after that, but a good while before Sadie found out you play marimba and we started our sessions together ..."

Celeste's reverse gazing hung up though, as her mind went to the event, completely discombobulating her telling. "Oh mercy. That created some gridlock. I wish you had been here then, Mare. Stuart masterminded the move for me. How he would've loved your help."

"Wait! What are you saying? You used to have a garage at St. Anne, and then when you sold your beaute, you moved the garage away somewhere?"

Celeste managed a nod.

"I always thought that was strange. Regoire having to park

around by the kitchen door. Stuart staying out on the street for everything but the heaviest loads. Delaney. You've always let her little work truck in though, right?"

"Heavens. You make it sound like I police the lane."

There was that side-pucker again.

"I merely preferred quiet confines. Once I let go of my Z24 ... I had no interest in becoming one of those elderly drivers whom parents tell their kids to watch out for ... I just liked the look of our gardens and St. Anne itself without that detached garage. It never did fit. And who in the world living by herself needs a two-car garage?"

Of course they both recognized with a look. Easily, Mare.

"But you know what happens to a garage without her car. It fills up. I didn't want that! I told Regoire he could have a tastefully attached garage built on the side but he never had an interest. I don't think. Do you know otherwise?"

"Ha. I don't know anything."

"Well you certainly know mechanics. Engineering in your way too. Now let's have a look see." And Celeste pushed back a sweet-smelling unpruned myrtle limb ...

Mare wasn't sure she was following Celeste.

"I don't know if we can make it this way," Celeste stopped, worn out anyway. "May I lean on you dear? Maybe after tea we can take my rig and wheel round Iverness to the boulevard."

Mare at least made an attempt to poke through the growth. "What are you wanting me to see Celeste?"

"It's the garage, dear. I moved the garage to this corner, facing the other way, naturally. Surely you've noticed it. You used to pedal by every day from down the coast."

"Celeste, that? That! I know that building, of course, but I thought it belonged to whoever owns the property to your south. Iverness does this jog of an approach to the boulevard. I guess I thought your property squared up to Harris. And all this overgrown corner, I didn't think it

18

belonged to you. ... Well, I knew you didn't want us going out this way, as that would invite others to cut across your property. I just never put the two together."

"When Mulch came I suggested he not bother restoring this far back. But we could. The building's not in bad shape. The renters kept it up."

"You say 'kept.' Is it empty?"

"Ah yes. I've not been in it since they moved on." Celeste laughed. "Actually I hadn't been in the building since I had it moved. I thought Bobby told me ..."

But again, Celeste chose trailing off, the prudent route. And Mare was more than full with thoughts of a shop to have picked up on Celeste's breach.

While Regoire tidied after their tea and tarts, then set about getting early prep underway for dinner, Thom volunteered to accompany Celeste and Mare the long way, out through the lane, around to Iverness and onto the Boulevard. So Regoire ushered Celeste down the hallway while Thom retrieved the wheelchair from where they'd left it outdoors, Regoire's hand squared at Celeste's back. "I'm right on your wavelength my dear. I took the liberty of planning dinner for all? How does a light steamed Rockfish with mussels on the side, a squash, what do you think ... Delicata," deciding for himself, "and your favorite mix of greens with balsamic dressing sound? I've had a sweet baguette in the works since morning anyway."

"You won't mind, Regoire? That would be so lovely."

"Stuart will bring by the seafood. I don't have time for a trip to the market myself, but my friends at the dock look out for me. They know what I will and what I won't bring home, so anyone there will give Stuart the very best they've got. I asked Stuart to stay, yes?"

"And Delaney?"

As Mare appeared from peeking at the gardens, Thom, ready with the wheelchair, overheard, "I phoned, left a message.

Celeste and Regoire puffed up as one, neither needing to voice that they were thinking 'Full sunroom again!'

Mare stepped back onto the Boulevard sidewalk then up to the corner of the building, peering in the farthest window too. She pulled a sleeve up over her hand, wiped a spot, but no luck seeing well. 'Something's not right,' she squinted towards Thom, but Thom, at a loss, had no response.

"Well you need to get inside! I'm so sorry I thought I had the correct key on my ring. Regoire will help me locate it, if not tonight, by morning. He's so good to throw an impromptu homecom ..." Again Celeste cut herself off, hoping too much that Mare would not bolt.

Chapter 3 ~ Discovered
fr Late Latin
discooperīre

"**Dinner,** Mare was most definitely present, Aggie perched on one knee, the two leaning into each other every now and then as conversation swirled around them.

"lblblbl," giggle giggle.

"lblblbl," more gigs from Aggie, accompanied by Mare's guttural huh-huhs.

Lorena spooned peas which Regoire had puréed with mint from the garden into Aggie's gig-gurgle. Mare did her best to encourage the swallow with a "blbl-blb"

Darned if 'Dimply Doodle' didn't very nearly slip out of Mare's mouth, but she grabbed the impulse in time to cut short such sweetie dribbling, and not entirely for Lorena's benefit either.

Mare was holding a steady intrigue over how it would work

to be back in the bounds of St. Anne. With comfortable detachment, Mare found it interesting that she was more curious than concerned.

After dinner Celeste checked with Regoire. Regoire had keys to every St. Anne lock, lined up and labeled right to the left inside la cuisine walk-in, easy as Regoire's pie to produce. Celeste gladly passed the garage key off to Mare so Mare and Delaney could go back, just the two of them, Delaney packing her wide-beam flashlight.

"I'd forgotten that there aren't any garage doors. Might be why it never clicked that this was a garage, let alone that it had come round from St. Anne's."

"If I'm remembering right, the renters did some renovation." Delaney shined the flashlight where the double doors had been. Shaking her head, "Yeah, look, you can see where they walled it, filling in siding rather than refacing the whole street front. Tacky," Delaney laughed. "I'm surprised Celeste didn't have them redo."

"I don't know if she knew."

Unlocking, Mare stepped over the threshold like she couldn't wait to own the place.

Right off Mare eyed what had to be a fake wall. "A grow room would have no natural light, but it would need a water source, need to be air tight here on a main road," feeling along the wall as she went. "Would have a thermostat, probably ultra white in there, most likely a humidifier but I imagine that left with the last occupants."

Delaney didn't say so but she was impressed with Mare's working knowledge. Not surprised though. Nor was she put off. "Clever," meaning the former occupants.

Just then Thom opened the front door.

"Come on in."

"On my way home. Was curious what you saw in here."

"Wow, I didn't know you picked up on that," is what Mare

said but what she had whizzing through her mind was 'this coming back is completely different than I'd thought' it would be.' She could hardly take in how many people were interested in ... Shuddering, she scruffled her hand through her hair, gave her skull a good squeeze-and-release, then took Thom by the arm. "Look. See how the interior's shorter than the outer building?"

"Hey. You spotted that by peering through the window? Well done. I hadn't, but I wanted to see what you saw." Thom gave a pat to the wall. "Well, you'll figure it out. Sorry, I need to get home. So great if this works out for you, Mare. Good night, Delaney. Hope to see you both again soon."

Delaney and Mare were left to look up and down the shop wall. First they felt along with their hands. No sign whatsoever of a door. No shelving or bookcase that could conceal an entry. Stumped, they did one of those funny double-takes back and forth to each other. 'Really clever.' Couldn't help marveling over the person or persons who had inhabited the building before.

On a second try, Delaney went from one end, Mare from the other. Nothing. There were six seams in the wall. Odd. Covered with wainscoting, though probably not termed exactly that as the finished battens were perpendicular to full ceiling height. Nicely painted, or they had been at one time.

Some instinct had Mare eyeing the pendant fixtures, an outmoded kind like upside-down bowls, hooding single bulbs and hanging on those old-fashioned rods through which the wires thread. Four lights in all. But one ...

"I've got it."

Mare grabbed a backless chair, the only loose item left in the shop, worthless except for reaching that light. She was able to reach, grasp, turn the bulb tight. "Watch this," Mare pulled the short chain.

And of course nothing happened.

"Duh. No power. What am I thinking. That's it all right though. I'll bet you ..."

"I'm not betting anything. I'll bet you got it," Delaney laughed at her own contradiction. "When power's on ..."

"It's not like Celeste to ..."

"You're right. She's usually more on top of her property. Like over on the cottage row, I know she knows what's what over there."

"She loves those cottages."

"This grow room, assuming that's what's here, must've been set up before the law changed. Wouldn't be any need for this now."

"Well, less need, depending on intent."

"True."

"Anyway, I'm going to want work space way more than I want a hidden room and if Celeste is willing to rent to me ... why don't you give me the low-down on what I need to watch out for in restoring to one usable space."

"Mare, seriously, I don't mind coming in some evening and

whacking this out with you. It'll only take us a few hours and you'd have a full garage. We can set it up however you want from the start." Delaney pulled out her iphone, popped into her calendar, "The weekend's fine, or tomorrow night would work."

"I want to. But more of me wants to not steamroll this. Just because I'm stoked ... Better we give everybody a chance to get used to the idea of me working over here. The weekend would be soon enough."

"That's great by me. Stuart's going to be busy most of Saturday."

"So, what? Are you and Stuart ... ?"

"Eh. We see each other almost every day. Taking it slow."

"That would be Stuart."

"Yes. But me too. Beginnings are so ... well, you know," nodding with approval around the garage too. "It's good to savor. We're taking our time." Delaney's face gave away more than her words.

28

"Sweet!" poking Delaney. "And how is seeing each other every day 'taking it slow'?"

Delaney didn't mind Mare enjoying herself.

And Mare was enjoying. Well before daylight? At the garage, tinkering. Or rather, she could feel the fun in that coming on soon. Until then, plenty to think through. Easy enough to give Celeste time for her coffee, breakfast. Nine or so she'd walk over to talk with Celeste about the electricity. Mare planned to make the call for hook-up, then go in, put down a deposit if necessary. She was set on being super clear: she'd be paying rent and taking care of her own utilities. They'd need to come to an agreement about materials for renovating the inside. Mare knew Celeste would want to participate, yet she didn't want to take advantage of nor play off Celeste's past regrets. Mare thought if she could look into Celeste's eyes, they'd both be able to rest assured.

Meantime, looking over the light hood again Mare remembered Celeste had started to say something about

29

Bobby. She'd have to ask. How did Celeste have anything to do with Bobby? It'd been ages since Bobby and Richie had cleaned up after the earthquake. Richie, Mare could understand since Sadie and Richie were together and in contact from San Francisco. But Richie's brother Bobby? What touch would Celeste have ...

"Hey!" Mare was more in the moment than she'd realized. It looked like the rod to that end light fixture was a different size than the others. Maybe the entire unit was meant to pull down. With only an inch of the ripped cord hanging from the light, allowing too little purchase to pull from the floor, she stepped up on the broken chair again and tried tugging down from the sides of the hood. Sure enough, the fixture gave way right into her hands. She kicked the chair out from under her as the hood dropped low enough that she could see the small electrical housing above the light itself, and under that cover a flip switch. "Haaaa."

Forgetting everything except fascination about how a panel might move, she pressed the switch. There it was, a

30

creak and a squeak and a portion of the wall began to shudder and shift, revealing a middle panel attached to what looked like custom-made super-long drawer slides, top and bottom, with a simple elbow inward onto the slides. No hinge. Just the panel itself swiveling a half inch into the room behind, then shooting straight to the east wall on the inside of the adjoining panel. Mare held the switch down until that section had completely receded.

'We sure should've tested an outlet instead of assuming the power was off just because a bulb was out. And me a fixer!' At her next thought, 'Delaney's going to love that' though, Mare caught up with herself once more. Stepping into the exposed room, electricity and even embarrassment took a back seat.

"No way!" Mare coughed. Then her hacking broke into all out choked laughter. "I can't believe it. No friggin way!" She pulled her cell out of her hip pocket. Not surprisingly, Mare carried a macho heavy duty old-school phone. Flip top. All kinds of tools and safety features, like shatter proof, waterproof, but with none of the smart phone capabilities. Still, it worked well for Mare.

"Delaney, are you at a job yet? You're going to want to see this."

"What is it? Baths?"

"If those are bath tubs, they're sure grody. Nope, the people who rented this place were growing ..." Mare wanted to see if Delaney would figure it out.

"Shrimp! Mare it's a mini shrimp farm."

"Yep. Fresh water shrimp. Or ... I don't know, it looks like they may have added the salt."

Pipes were still in place feeding into the tanks from the bottom, some overhead, linking one tank to the next.

"I can see why, whoever managed this operation was going to replace the baths," Delaney screwed up her face, "or the tanks, if you will, at their new location. Assuming this was a test run. My gosh it's going to take renting some ... a jackhammer that'll whack horizontally?

33

This …" Delaney gripped the rigid tank wall, "it's an earthen base, looks like, but there's a chemical binder of some sort." Tugging at it, "Feels like a cross between concrete and steel almost. Going to be a …"

"A bi..!" Mare threw away the last half of an expletive too, knowing how possible it was that Celeste, or Lorena with Aggie, could show up any time. Holding her tongue would be a fair trade-off for getting to work near that little one.

"But why would they need an undercover operation?"

Mare was on it, following the water lines … under a wall … so she had to pivot, back out through the front door, Delaney close behind … and around the building … to "Well water! Zero expense for the water cycling system. Zero fees for licensing. Zero bother from health inspectors."

"This is the craziest thing."

"Ha! You don't know crazy," Mare certified, "till you've been down in the Bay for a while. But yeah, this is borderline shocker all right, for right here on the back side of St. Anne. Wonder what Celeste's going to think."

"I guess we can tell her?"

They did over coffee in the sunroom.

"Heavens, what one doesn't know."

None of them could piece together why those renters had been so secretive about growing shrimp. Delaney's scan on her phone revealed little. Their most believable speculation was that it'd been some sort of pilot program attempting to breed giant prawns for commercial market.

"A white tail disease could have wiped them out," Regoire offered while filling their cups.

"It doesn't matter now."

"You don't mind if we dismantle the tanks?"

"Heavens Mare, I wish you would."

"And about eliminating that room altogether ..." Delaney,

ever clear with property owners, didn't want to fall short on double checking that detail.

"As long as the two of you are willing, whatever you need to do, do it. Can you get help in hauling away the tank material? I'd have you just crush and spread it behind the building, if you even could, but you know Lorena. One whiff of a 'white tail disease' and she'll be high tailing it. You'll never have Aggie visiting your shop. It better all go."

"Dump run's easy. Chet likes to get in on those." Delaney squeezed Celeste's hand. "Well, I'm off now." Calling through, "Thanks for the coffee, Regoire. Celeste." Then, "See you this weekend, Mare."

In the end it was Regoire who took Mare aside, and without even realizing, helped clear her way forward. While Celeste was engaged in her after meal ministrations, Regoire poured himself and Mare a third cup of coffee. The honey-creamed dark roast along with Regoire's offhand suggestion sent Mare spinning. Enough so that she punched in a text to Delaney to see if she could swing by one more time whenever it fit in her schedule.

"Regoire had this idea ... of me living here too, at least while I'm getting underway. I don't know why I hadn't thought of it. The room's hermetically sealed, so to speak. I could use this small side for living, and I wouldn't be breathing bearing grease or gasoline in my sleep."

"If you were the kind of person who needs a buffer between home and work, I'd say forget it," Delaney laughed, taking stock of the small space. "But for you!" Delaney could see "counter for hotplate and toaster oven, daybed ... shower installation, all doable. This could make a great studio apartment. Plus, that secret door is just so cool. I want to see if Stuart can figure it out."

"He won't."

"I know."

Saturday, before they got going on the shrimp tanks,

Delaney took a moment to size up the room again. "You know, if you want we can knock out a back door and window." She thumped a few times, "Anywhere here ..." locating the studs, "and here. Sure would make the space feel bigger. I can get ahold of a really fun and functional Dutch door."

"Heck, do you have the right saw with you? Let's do it!"

Mare always did get a little ahead of herself. But Delaney knew about a deal on a recycled Dutch door and on an 8-pane window. Knew the items were at Re-Store too because she'd taken them out of a home and deposited them herself ... which is why she wouldn't hesitate to cut through the back wall. She had the dimensions recorded right there on her phone. They just wouldn't be able to get to the items till after Delaney finished work on Monday.

Didn't matter to Mare. Soon they had two good-sized holes through the back of what would become her mini living quarters. Ergo, Mare had committed to spending the next nights on a borrowed cot, sleeping out in the main part of the building. With the secret door open she could keep an eye on both sides. Delaney had gone along with Mare's impulse mostly because the taller opening made it so much easier when they got to hauling out the chunks of debris. She could back right up to the doorway, without the impediment of a door.

Mare could fall asleep anywhere. And ordinarily she was immune to excitement interfering with sleep. 2AM Sunday morning though, in a 'to heck with it' turning one too many times, Mare got up and finished dousing vinegar over the stray remains left from the demolition, wiping everything clean. Then she took measurements, cut the headers, Mowgli's "I'm Good" playing full out from her dated boombox. With the shop being on the Boulevard, Mare could work all night whenever she wanted and no one would hear her power tools ... or see her playing marimba of sorts on her eventual workbench, drumming as she was sure to with whatever she had at hand.

Now Delaney ... she would not have left unfinished trim around the door jamb. And Delaney would definitely have detailed baseboards along the walls, pre-staining, sinking the nails with her nail set, puttying the holes, swiping smooth and sanding to a nice touch-up finish. But differences among friends can extend a long way and it matter not a whit. Delaney did help those first evenings. Window and door quickly installed.

Mare for her part was eager to get on with 'real work.' To that end, having willingly left her old bench with Mulch, she built a heavy new workbench in one bay. Next she threw up shelving along two walls. Then extended the back access, carving a pull-in for her small pickup out of the encroaching buckthorn beside the shop as well as making a smaller spot by the back door. Yes, there'd be room enough if she ever got a motorbike, with plenty of overflow parking along the street.

As soon as Mare had the shop bare bones workable, she picked up a metal cash box on her way to City Hall.

Okay so it was secondhand and only a cash box by stretch. The metal flip-top had originally been used for fishing tackle, but Mare had her eye on profit, as well as purpose which only partially involved profit, way more than looks or shoulds. She liked what she saw of the business license requirements too. Only one short form and two twenties.

In a blink, word would be spreading out from St. Anne's. Mare would not only have small appliance repairs arriving legitimately through the front door, she'd have assorted appliances showing up out back. And as soon as she would repair one of the odd oldies, sometimes donating off to the help center, another would show up just like it. For the time being Mare opted to let slide the dumping service she had inadvertently created. In the recycling process, she was sure to pick up the occasional rare part in good enough shape to reuse for a relieved customer at some point down the way. Her shelving would serve to keep all in order.

Of course that first mid-week morning when Mare officially opened, St. Anne's little family was on the spot.

"Good guess! You are right," Mare greeted them. "First thing first, I got the toaster fixed."

"First thing first," Lorena high-kneed it around the workbench, Chet hepping behind, and straining a bit as he held Aggie aloft.

"Crrkkrkkcrrk"

Mare wagged her nose at Aggie. First things first.

It seemed the family was on an about-face though, so Mare headed them off. "Lorena, I want your approval on something."

Relieved, Chet stood Aggie on the workbench.

Lorena patted the toaster. "We're taking our parade home for pop tarts, Mare."

"It'll only take a minute ... it's about Aggie."

"Second thing second," Chet tried. He couldn't have

gotten more of a response if he'd simply fallen on the floor himself. As it was, Aggie toppled into him so they both nearly bit it.

Mare eyed her new wonder. 'Now how does she know to go for effect?' More than surprisingly Mare had been giving considerable thought to Aggie. And Mare, wasn't 'a little kid person' at all.

Mare sure did not see herself spending a lot of time at St. Anne's, not in the loose ends way she had in years past. Oh, she definitely planned to schedule drumming sessions. The marimba desire had not subsided. Plus, she knew how good it was for Celeste to keep active in body and mind. She wanted to be there for Celeste in those regards. But otherwise, she wasn't going to be mooching off Regoire for meals. And she wasn't going to be the resident babysitter like some rudderless high school student. Being single, one had to cut clear parameters.

Still, 'reality' had shifted so much from what Mare had imagined before her return. That first moment she and

Aggie met, Mare knew … something. Something about that kid got to her.

She could see herself giving Aggie's parents a break whenever they wanted. Only taking care of Aggie would have to be on her terms, in her way. She could almost picture Aggie hanging out at the shop with her. But of course a fix-it shop was generally no place for a toddler, and not for some years to come either. So, Mare put her mind to it just like she would any fix-it and hit on how it could work.

Instead of locking up all the harmful items, she'd do it the other way around and lock Aggie away from everything that could hurt her. No, no, not how that sounds. Mare wanted Aggie to be with her at the same time as Aggie was kept safe. So she had designed a folding fence, an accordion-type containment area that she could move from place to place. Of course Mare would gravitate to wood, but giving it more thought, she switched to plastic, power-washable outdoors, as needed. The fencing, not Aggie.

She told Lorena and Chet, "It will be Aggie's Work Area," knowing that Lorena would go for a proper name and accordingly might overlook the enclosure's likeness to a playpen. Aggie's would have a roll-out floor, a vinyl cushioned curl-up comfort spot, an open chest with real things from the shop ... chosen for absence of sharp edges and chemical compounds. A radio, for instance, like Mare's, super old school, hand-held, working of course, possibly red, and a credit-card swiper with a bundle of old cards.

Yes, it was going to be somewhat of a hassle and maybe she'd tire. But in this day-dreaming stage Mare really dug the idea of moving the fence so she could stand inside and work at a table, with Aggie right behind her, yet inside the fence herself. Eventually ... maybe ... yeah, out in the future, Mare had images of Aggie being able to safely learn her way around the shop without needing to be penned up. There was also the issue of being right on the Boulevard, with a door opening for shop customers, so containment would be essential for a good long while.

Lorena gave Mare a thumbs up without asking for Chet's input which was fine by Chet. That was all the blessing Mare needed to set up Aggies's Work Area however she thought best. Lorena motioned towards the path, onward to try out their restored toaster.

Chet, doing his usual in-step act, packing Aggie in various silly positions, made Lorena's abrupt U-turn right on her heels.

"Ow!" Lorena limped back in, "Mare, what's all that piled up out back? It stinks! You're not leaving it there, are you? What is it?"

"Shrimp tanks, Lorena." How hard could it be after all to just give Lorena straight answers.

"I didn't see any toy wheels ... or armor."

Holding off an eye roll, "Not shrimpy, Lorena," and coughing away a laugh, "not that kind of tank."

"I don't see anything but a stinky mess."

"I know. It wouldn't all fit in Delaney's pickup. I'll be hauling away the rest in mine. Real soon. I'm counting on your help, Chet. That be all right?"

Chet gave Mare a pinched thumbs up as he shifted Aggie again. "'rena are we staying or going?"

"I want to hear about this shrimp business, Mare."

"Very good, Lorena. That's what it was, a shrimp business."

Lorena assured Chet with a glance that his waiting was worth it.

But Mare stopped before even starting. She'd come to the end of straight answering, with the inevitable roundabouts, for the moment anyway. "I'll tell you the whole story. Remind me."

When Bobby opened the door, the bell dinged, stretching his smile even wider than he already had going. Then as he crossed the threshold a colored light commenced blinking, running through the rainbow spectrum, holding five full seconds at violet. Not that Mare particularly liked rainbows, except that they'd be cool for the times Aggie hung out with her, or so the preschool enthusiasts might say. No. The rainbow doorblinger simply flashed Mare's affinity for gizmos and gadgets. She'd built and installed the welcome light when it became clear that the bell wasn't always getting her attention. Fairly often she'd be focused with a power tool or testing some clattery appliance, so didn't hear the bell. The lights helped alert her that she wasn't alone.

When Bobby entered the shop ... bell, blinker and all ... he shouted out above her grinder, "Hey, you're looking

48

good. How are you?"

Mare flicked the switch, off.

"Holy crap, Bobby, how are you?" Mare had flirted with Bobby when he clearly wasn't available. The instant she saw how he grinned so big at her greeting, question marks shot up like Lorena's pop tarts. Without missing a beat Mare switched to circumspect. Not a contrived move but a gambit nonetheless. For emphasis, Mare set down her tool and edged round the corner till she had the full length of the workbench between them. "How's Bountiful? Weren't you and she ...?"

A fraction of puzzlement flashed across Bobby's face, but there was nowhere for it to lodge. Bobby was fine. He needed nothing from Mare. Nice enough to have her in town again.

Bobby rested a foot on an overturned bucket. "She's good, I think. I'm great. Bountiful followed Richie and them down to the Bay."

"Richie and Sadie."

"Yeah yeah, and another of our friends. I don't think you knew him."

"Oh."

"The guy who rented this shop."

"Oh!"

"Yeah, it was kinda. But better now. I'm just here. Workin'." He came close to toeing his boot onto the floor, but pulled out of that too. No more tripping into old rabbit holes. "Hey I'm glad you're back."

Unusual to hear a knock from out at the studio door. Mare went to answer leaving Bobby dangling.

"We got yer path all cleared there Mare. Yous don't mind if Chet and I gives your building a little color, do ya?"

And there came Chet, pushing St. Anne's largest wheel barrow full of six good-sized Agapantha.

"Oh Mulch!"

Neither being huggers, Mare skipped the embarrassment and stepped right out to steady the careening wheelbarrow and guide it around the side of the building.

Through the window Bobby caught what looked like cartoon silhouettes filling up the frame. He shot out the shop door to see what was up.

"In front, Mulch, where others can enjoy them too don't you think. I love Agapantha."

"I's thought that was one of yer flowers."

Bobby dove right in, relieved Mulch of his shovel and set about helping Chet dig up two swatches of the scruffy parking strip while Mare took Mulch inside to show him around. The overture did not go unnoticed indoors.

"Nice fella that Bob," Mulch rated.

"He's just stopped by to say hello. This is the first I've seen of him."

What was Mare doing, feeling like she had to justify her moves? And with Mulch?

Conrad, one of the UPS guys, set off the blinger.

"You need a whistle with that, Mare. Maybe a whistle's what you've ordered here?"

"Funny, Con, just send me some customers would ya. Next time you come you can see that suspension part you're carrying in place where it belongs in a mower I inherited. Unless I sell it first, that is."

"Now you're doing lawn mower repair as well?"

"Fixin it. That's what I'm about. And building new when I'm not busy fixin. Either way, send me customers."

"Interesting," as he headed out. "Bobby man, how's it!" Mare could hear through the open door, "Sorry about Bounti, man."

"Nah. Everything's cool. Last I heard, Richie said she

52

was in Seattle ... or St. Louis." Bobby intensified shovel to dirt.

"Take care, man."

When Mulch finished his look round the shop, he gave Bobby a half-nod, with a 'just mind your p's and q's' squeeze on his shoulder as he stepped round to help Chet heel in the blooms. Bobby hoped they were closing the door on the past part of that topic, for good.

It's good to know these things.

Chapter 6 ~ Acquiesced

fr Latin
acquiēscere

If you're like me when you're reading along and something comes up that you don't quite follow, carrying on is a bit of a wobbly-do until the question in mind gets cleared up, answered. So, perhaps you're with Mare on 'What's with Aggie's arm?'

Let's take a look. A quick peek while Lorena's out for the afternoon. With Chet. Errands, by bus. Aggie is with them, which is all the better. No need riling Lorena with us peering in close. All Mare has wanted since she got back was a few more details.

First we have to decamp. Back to when Stuart was researching, Delaney feeding him links. But even before that, when the unnamed baby was still in utero, Stuart and Delaney got stuck down a side avenue: out of what beliefs does a person make those huge decisions based on prenatal test results. Neither could submit with assurance what they would do if they encountered an abnormality while their baby was in the womb. Luckily, all at St. Anne, for the time being, were well past that intersection.

During the pregnancy, and disregarding Celeste, Lorena would not comply with even one test that involved the baby. Somehow Lorena viewed her own blood as cut off from the child she carried. All the better, nurses said on the side. And no one felt it would serve anything to shine a light on the Lorena/baby connecting apparatus, so Lorena did have standard blood work, and with no abnormalities showing up.

Post birth the doctors were overjoyed ... well, relieved, which is after all a doctor's version of joy. Even with Aggie entering the world on the beach, all signs pointed to a very healthy baby.

It wasn't until about the sixth month that the St. Anne ménage began to notice. One after another they were asking themselves, 'Is her arm all right?' 'Is she favoring that arm?' 'Am I seeing things or is her right arm not as long as her left?' All muted, mind you.

It was closer to nine months, with Aggie already pulling herself up ... plenty of power in those little legs ... that Celeste asked Regoire outright. "There could be a case made for 'hardly shorter,' very much so for 'hardly noticeable.' What do you think?"

"Whether it's noticeable or not isn't the point."

Subject finally opened, Regoire and Celeste conferred, two days running. But Regoire soon reached his limit.

"Celeste, we're going over and over the same ground. Agreed, we don't know about longterm range of motion. Nor about her eventual full use of both arms. And most importantly, 'What if anything is this a precursor to?' That's what Thom brought up last night."

Celeste shrunk in panic. Regoire's next comment did nothing to reassure.

"Lorena has us in such a bind. Now every time I see

Aggie, I'm asking myself, 'Should godfathers have it looked at?'"

"You know what Lorena would say. She'd have a fit."

"Exactly. That's the bind!"

"I wish Sadie was here. A physical therapy of sorts would be so natural with our Sadie." In slow motion, Celeste unfurled one arm out in front of her. "Surely Sadie could help with extensions ..." matching her one arm with the other. "Should I see if Sadie can come home for a visit?"

"I believe this needs to be addressed here and now. It was one thing when Lorena was pregnant. Now the child's real, and Thom and I are godfathers," with a bit more anguish than he meant to let out.

But crashing in the kitchen cut their conversation. Regoire half raised out of his chair to dash ... when he realized, sank back down. That was not an accidental pan-slipping-from-hand.

Celeste went wide-eyed at what came next. Must surely

have been more lids slapping the wall. Spinning across the floor. Together Regoire and Celeste sank, desperately disappointed. Disappointed in themselves for not being more careful.

A moment later, from their huddle they heard ... kitchen door flung open with a thunk, footsteps heading the opposite direction, and what sounded like an exit out the front with one of those fully intentioned slam-bams.

Mare hadn't been on hand of course, but Celeste had recounted to Delaney in due time. Delaney caught Mare up to speed all these weeks later.

"Gosh I've been wondering. I wasn't sure if I was seeing right, but I didn't want to bring it up."

"Oh yeah, it's shorter. By how much, who knows. I'm pretty sure no one's measured."

"There are various kinds of bullies. Sometimes I think Lorena's more of an emotional bully than Celeste."

Delaney, pulled back, surprised. "But doesn't love ..."

Mare's turn to recoil.

"I know I know. Poor word choice, 'love' so carelessly and overused. But what other is there? That's what makes these dilemmas, these impossible predicaments bearable. Even when they won't speak of it, love supersedes everything between those two. Lorena and Celeste, I mean. And now 'the three' have formed the generations of St. Anne's as if that were always meant to be."

Not long after Lorena's blow up in the kitchen, when Celeste was down for a nap, Aggie napping too, Lorena had sought out Regoire.

"What would they do, to find out about her arm?"

"We're not at all sure, Lorena. They'd have to run tests."

"How? On What?"

"Well, they'd first do a baseline."

"I've already told her about baseball and it's all written down for when she can read."

"That's good, Lorena." Regoire turned away to compose himself. "The kind of baseline they're going to do …"

Seeing Lorena bristle he searched again for a way to begin. "If a parent wanted some answers from the medical profession, first there would be a diagnostic exam. The parent is always there while the doctor feels the arm and shoulder and chest to see how the bones are lined up, and that doctor would listen to the heart, and maybe gently press into her abdomen." As the light in Lorena's eyes faded to absent, Regoire moved on into 'consultation,' touching Lorena's wrist as he continued, getting her back with him. "The doctor would write down what he found from the exam. Then the nurse would take a sample of blood from the child and they'd send that out to a lab to get analyzed. A laboratory," Regoire corrected himself. "The notes that the doctor made and the results of the blood work would form the baseline to which all follow-up examinations would be compared."

"You mean it wouldn't be settled what they plan to do in one exam?"

"No, I'm afraid not. Though we're not trained like the doctors, we have been researching ..." Again with the bristles. "Mostly Stuart, and Delaney if she thought of something for Stuart to check out." No need to tell Lorena that Celeste had been online every day since they first began talking 'Aggie's arm.' "We can see, there is probably no straightforward diagnosis that a doctor will pull out of a hat. If Aggie had been injured in birth ..."

Lorena took two quick steps back. But an inch from fleeing.

"No, Lorena, I don't mean she should have been! I mean babies whose mommies had a hard labor, nothing at all like yours, the doctor could tell you right off what could be done with exercises and all, to get the arm to growing again. But that's not the case with Aggie. She had an easy birth," stressing with a repeat. "You and Aggie did really well. So now, to find out what has caused one arm to slow in its growth after she'd been growing just fine, it could take a while for the doctors to rule out all the things it's not."

"You're saying, the doctors would talk with Chet and me and Aggie about what could be wrong with her?"

"They may, yes."

"Well Regoire, good! You've answered my question." She reached up and hugged Regoire around the neck.

Then, even as she clearly was, Regoire pleaded "Don't go. Lorena, tell me, what did I answer?"

"It's simple, Regoire. There's nothing wrong with Aggie. I don't want her … I don't even want Chet to start thinking of something being wrong with her. And even if the doctors didn't put it that way, if I told them 'no way!' beforehand somehow, going in one time and then another and another to run around that baseline … Aggie's going to wonder if something is wrong. Chet will for sure. He's already thinking something because this afternoon I told him to go home and take a nap. See, as soon as we start looking at Aggie in a maybe 'oh no!' way, all kinds of 'oh no's' are going to come out … out of … well, everybody here, for one! One pool, one school of kettles."

Lorena finished with a feeble smile.

Would doctors have been able to determine anything more than Stuart and Delaney had? Well. of course they should, but clearly professionals maintained no fast-lane freeway. Celeste kept on it herself, limited now to looking online from her bedchamber up in the tower. She couldn't conduct investigations on her laptop in the sunroom as there was no telling when Lorena might pop up behind her. The volume of information was overwhelming, so eventually Celeste gave up trying to figure it out. Safer to rely on Stuart's summaries.

From what he and Delaney could piece together, the cartilage in Aggie's right upper arm was not forming into bone at the same rate as in her left. If she had achondroplasia, one would expect both arms to be involved. It didn't seem to be related to one of the diseases that crimp the functioning of the liver and muscles either. That was good. Stuart was most intrigued by the possibility that Lorena had ingested lead in her early years in foster care ... older homes on the coast being prime storage bins for lead ... and that toxin could've passed on to Aggie. But why curtailed growth of one limb would be the result, Stuart had no idea. Nor did he have confidence that doctors would either. Stuart and Delaney shared their information with Celeste and Regoire, and through Regoire to Thom, but with little enthusiasm.

In Lorena's mind, and therefore in Chet's as well, the source could have easily been a crab with one pincer longer than the other, passing by at Aggie's birth. Lorena and Chet talked out this possibility between them-selves, accepting, whatever the case.

And what did it matter? To Lorena, not a bit.

Eventually all at St. Anne let it be. Regoire and Thom never had another discussion about having Aggie tested, not with Lorena. And certainly not with Chet who would've been troubled knowing how it would upset 'rena, to whom he deferred anyway on (most things) Aggie.

Call it what you will. Gross negligence. Child endangerment. Who is to say, and at what point will judgment be laid? Would whatever outcome of a longitudinal exam bring greater benefit to Aggie, in the end, than that bestowed by her iron-willed mother who saw unequivocally: nothing wrong with Aggie, nothing needing fixing.

And anyway, Aggie's arm wasn't significantly shorter ... and what if it was? That she was far from grown did hang in the private spaces of the heart for the elder lot at St. Anne. Lorena though had already shown Aggie how to even out her arms.

"Palms together, like patty cake," she instructed. "Thumbs up, and stretch your arms straight out." The next part Lorena helped Aggie with, at least the first times. "If ever you want you can make your fingertips match."

Lorena would hold her daughter's shoulders in a light grasp from above and turn Aggie's torso gently to Aggie's left, thereby making it so the fingertips lined quite up. "See!"

And Aggie would, sharing her momma's glee.

But that didn't stop Celeste from, years to come, installing a monkey bars in the garden, the old-fashioned kind where a youngster hung from two hands and swung, hand stretching to hand stretching, across. No one ever stated a reason. Everyone just enjoyed. Aggie most of all.

"Celeste, *I don't want to alarm you.*"

Celeste had answered the phone when no one else was at hand. Glad she had, "Yes, after hours is fine. I'll wait for you in the sunroom. Just come on in."

Mare was keeping her shop open later, then later yet, as it seemed many customers preferred to stop in on their way home from work, often with DIY questions, some of which required home visits on the spot. She changed her Hours Open sign accordingly.

When Stuart suggested she was being too gracious in her service, Mare countered, "You're one to talk. If I ever approach your delivery standards, Stuart ... All you do above and beyond the call! And not just for Celeste."

"Don't kid yourself, it's selfish on my part. Getting to be a help to those who appreciate it ... I'm the one who benefits."

"Well then, good reason to keep on in the direction I'm going. Besides, the other day when I got to this man's house, his dishwasher was smoking! If I hadn't followed him home ... he'd just stopped in to tell me how he'd inserted an alligator clip to make a connection that'd burned out ... he might've lost his whole house."

So Mare got to Celeste's well after dinner. Regoire had left her a plate in the warming oven with a note taped to Celeste's sleeve: 'Mare ⟶ oven.'

"Celeste, thank Regoire for me." Big smile. "And thank you. This cannelloni hits the spot."

"Spinach and parmesan. Of course. I will. Now what did you want to tell me."

"Do you remember Claire?" waiting through a bite. "Sorry to bring her up. I know we'd all like to forget her altogether."

"Of course I remember. How the best massages I've ever had could come through the fingers of such an underhanded, self-serving ..." Celeste cut herself off. "Is this just a trip back in time or has she shown up again?"

"I can't be sure yet, which is why I wanted to see what you know. I think that doctor she worked for, or was in love with or whatever, I think he might have come round to the shop."

"Heavens! We'll need to tell Regoire. I reported that man and I'll press for a restraining order if I have to."

"No, I don't think that's called for, not yet anyway. I thought you might remember his name."

"Sadie will. Let me email her. I'd like a little sherry if you don't mind getting it, Mare. Get yourself ... those little glasses in the case. That scoundrel's not going to steal my sound sleep again."

Midmorning, midweek Mare rang up St. Anne's a second time.

With Regoire's long strides he could have made it round

the block in five, or out the path probably in three and a half. He could not countenance that man, so much so that he hopped in his Audi Coupe and was at Fix It in two, calling Thom on his car phone as he drove round.

Still, the doc had left.

"He says he's doing a study. That's all it is. He could ask Aggie questions from here and wouldn't bother anyone at St. Anne's."

Regoire looked ready to pounce even without the doctor on the premises.

"But Regoire I told him no!"

"Oh." Visibly, muscles relaxing. "Bien."

"I'm not any more comfortable with that man than you are. And the request itself, what does that imply about Chet and Lorena that a doc wants to study up their offspring! It's gross. I told Celeste that I'd seen him once. I'm sure if she knew he'd been around again, she'd be all 'He's way out of line.'"

Celeste could easily pick up on Lora's comments as Lora popped in now and then from 'the other side.' If Mare or Regoire had Celeste's antenna, Lora's 'not by half' might have tickled their funnies. Lora was only flitting through anyway, on route from hovering in London. She wasn't even going to stop over for a 'sit-down' with Celeste, though she did flutter Celeste's coif giving them both shivers of a good sort. Lora peeked in on Lorena and Aggie too, the real reason for her periodic 'fly-by's. Now if Thom had been at Fix It ... he might have chuckled out loud, even slapped his leg in a way Lora couldn't as he and Celeste did share that ability to tune in, hear the dead.

Regoire was focused on what he could see, or at least could arrange for keeping track of. "Thom can get away, right at noon. I told him to come straight here, but really I've got to get back if we're going to ... I'm gratified you agree, better to not have this conversation under Celeste's nose. We can tell her eventually, but there's no need right yet. I think I'll not bother Thom with another call now either. Can you simply tell him in detail what the man said and where he stood ... whatever you can remember. We have learned, if nothing else, to document everything. "

"Sure. Oh and Sadie emailed back. Dr. Lipsack. Sadie said that's not quite right but something close."

"Lipsacsh."

"Yeah, that's it. That's what he said. Strange man. No. More like disquieting. I can't figure why he gives me the shudders, but, yeck, right when he opened the door. Chills."

"Mare, if he comes in again ask what it will take for him to leave us alone. No more contact. No more querying. I've had it with this ..."

"Regoire ..."

"You know very well I'm not going to get physical with the 'doctor.'" Mare couldn't help a laugh, trying to picture Regoire taking a swing at anyone. Regoire pretended she hadn't. "But I will ask Thom to step in. Thom's bailiwick after all."

"Thom did come round, took notes, took care best he could. Then he was off to join Regoire and Celeste for lunch.

Mare never knew through one day or week if or when she would have company. One of the plusses of running a shop. Kept things interesting. UPS Conrad liked to linger. As did the old guy from two blocks down the street, those two blocks being a stretch for him, so Mare found a comfy folding Captain's chair which she either set outside or in, weather depending. Cap, as she got to calling him, could sit a spell before he headed back home. A co-worker from her old mechanic's shop stopped in too when he was over on Mare's side of town.

When Bobby dropped by next he could hardly get through the door.

"Whaa?" Mare moved to help him, laughing.

And he barely made it to the counter with the stack of appliances. "I asked the guys on my crew - what a bunch of lazy buggers. Or maybe they're just nowhere near as smart or handy as you."

"What have you got?"

"I had them tag with their name and cell number. When you see what needs doing, give a call, you know, just if you run into big expense on whatever part's needed. Then they can either give you a green light or ... I'll come by and pick up whatever's junk."

Mare chuckled some more, "I'll have a look. Thanks for the business ... I think."

"I hope it's not a waste of your time. I've got my aunt checking in with her choir members. We'll space out spreading the word so we don't pile you up too much.

Mare grinned. "Bring 'em on. There's no too much."

"Okay! So long then," Bobby left without a backward look.

Was he playing coy?

Mare didn't have long to ponder.

"Mare," the bell dinging, light flashing, "I need a sifter. One of those old kind where you crank the handle."

Lorena hobbled into the shop, Aggie at her knee, Aggie's right arm clamped round Lorena's leg.

Mare winked as if to say 'I like your slow-down speed control.' Then Mare bent to Aggie's level, "rrkr rrkr"

"rrkr rrkrrrh"

"I know what you mean, Lorena. I'll keep my eye out."

"lblblbl" Aggie went on.

"It's for Aggie." Lorena shook her leg, adding hiccups to Aggie's giggle.

Mare disengaged Aggie's grip on Lorena with a wordless offering of a floppy dog. As Aggie reached, Mare lifted her into Aggie's Work Area.

"I'd keep my eye out just as well for you as I would for Aggie. And vice versa."

"I don't need vices or verses," Lorena's hand moved involuntarily along the surface of Mare's workbench. She pulled it back, sensing something, kneading her fingers. "Do you have any Pyrex bowls though?

"What are you going to make? Pyrex bowls and sifters …"

"They're not the same."

Mare looked Lorena in the eye, 'obviously.'

"Mare, you're so funny."

Mare stopped herself from returning to her repairs. She'd figured out Celeste's trick. Giving Lorena her full attention was the only way to lift their interchanges into comprehensible.

"The sifter is for cornmeal. As soon as I get everything I need, I'm going to let Aggie have cornmeal playtime. It's like sand play in preschools … only it's cornmeal. Chet and I are going to get a 5-pound bag today. And some measuring cups and spoons that are just for Aggie.

76

Stainless steel, Stuart says, ones that are made in the U S of A. Because she's still going to put some things in her mouth and we want everything good produced."

"Yeah, I agree about made in USA. I imagine I can find a sifter for you. Those oldies were made here in the states, back when we still had factories. Midwest likely."

"I don't care which state it was made in."

"I know. I know. I'll keep a look out. What else did you say?"

"Pyrex bowls." Impatient. Lorena repositioned herself so she was between Aggie and Mare. "Medium-small size."

"lblblbl"

Obliging, Mare answered Lorena first, "Pyrex? Are you sure?" Then to Aggie, "lblblb-rrkr bb"

"rkrrkr bb rkr" Aggie squealed.

Mare tucked a hand around Aggie's head. Aggie sank onto her cushion, wrapping the floppy dog around her right arm.

"Aggie would do better with stainless steel wouldn't she? Like the measuring set you're getting her. Pyrex has good glass bowls all right but there's no getting around it, they break."

"Mare. Aggie's not going to play with the bowls. We're going to bake in them."

"Oh, mixing bowls!" turning back to her work. "Sure."

"No, Mare."

Exasperation worked well in Lorena's tool kit. Mare set down her screwdriver again.

"Aggie and I are going to bake bread."

Mare waited. Knowing that the obvious go-round through bread pans wasn't going to be necessary. If she stuck with listening, before long she'd be approaching the ease with which Celeste follows Lorena. And Chet.

"Must be a recipe I haven't seen yet."

"You want to see! I'll bring it. I'll show you. The advertisement said it's the easiest bread recipe ever. And I thought that maybe if I got Aggie going early Regoire would let her help him in la cuisine ..." she trailed off with what sounded like 'more than he has me.'

"That's going to be so cool, Lorena. Let me know ... Oh, well. You need the bowls first, right? Well when you get the bowls then let me know. I'd love a sample slice."

"I'm not sure if we're going to slice it, Mare. Chet and I haven't decided."

"O - kay ..."

"They call it peasant bread and the dough goes in the bowls and that's what you bake it in."

Sure enough, waiting out the questions, the answer would come round eventually.

"So with peasant bread you're thinking ..." Mare motioned pulling pieces apart.

Lorena reached out and hugged her. Awkward. Both. Still, quite like a hug.

"Would you like me to show you how to weave a basket? Then you could put the bread in a basket after it cools and break pieces off for people to reach in ..."

Lorena turned on her heel, dinging out the door.

"Chet! Chet!" hurrying down the empty pathway. "We're going to make baskets! Bread baskets!"

Without even looking behind, Mare slid a string of well-sanded PVC pipe slices and a mounted dowel in what she knew were Aggie's waiting hands. "She'll be back." But Aggie didn't need the assurance. The pipe sections and dowel clattered about in her play platform. Mare and Aggie were used to this, content. Chet, Lorena, someone from St. Anne would return for Aggie.

Then there was Bobby next day again. Lora, for one, was getting the picture. Back again herself, Aggie let out her "grrng" as the door opened, lights flashed.

"Hi Pumpkin!" Bobby began unwrapping a bite-size Tootsie roll and before Mare could get out her "Bobby,

You know she's not ..." Aggie had it clamped so hard in her mouth, there'd be no getting it out. Bobby and Aggie 'had chocolate drool coming out their eyeballs,' or so Mare planned to tell Lorena ... hoping though that they didn't get found out.

"That'll keep the kid occupied for a minute. I wanted to show you something."

He pulled a copy of a magazine article out of his jacket pocket.

"Have you ever heard of a water clock?"

"Where did this come from?"

"How's that tasting there, Sweet Cheeks?" as he got a paper towel and wiped Aggie's actual drool.

Mare picked right up on what Bobby hadn't answered. Scowled at him good.

"Look Mare. If I'd started out with ... if I'd told you ..."

"Well why don't you tell me now."

"It's nothing. And it's not her fault. Celeste and I had gotten together a while back, yeah. Because I brought by a gift from Richie 'n Sadie."

Mare wasn't softening a bit.

"See how you get. And if I had begun with 'Celeste and I were talking about you,' you would have got all bristly. You know you would, right? You are right now. You can't deny it."

Mare turned to fiddle with a loose wire on a toaster oven, biting the inside of her mouth a teeny bit so he wouldn't see her smile. "So this water clock here ..." She plunked down, picked up the magazine article again, "this new interest in an ancient water clock was your idea?"

"We'd all been talking about it. How cool it is. It came from a class Richie was taking. It wasn't so much Celeste's idea as our general opinion."

"Ours?"

"You know. Regoire and ..." Bobby sat next to her.

82

"Thom? Thom was in on this too?"

"Mare, you're getting the 'this' blown up way bigger than it was. I'd say forget it except that I think you're going to like the idea itself."

Bobby actually reached out and rested his hand on Mare's thigh, only slightly and super briefly. Mare hadn't flinched nor had she pulled away. Holding eye contact Bobby went on, "When Richie told me, and we got to talking, right off everybody thought 'Mare could build that.' Then Celeste and I looked for a picture online after I'd told them at St. Anne ... It was Richie told me ..." Bobby shrugged at his jumble of words, cupped his hands with two thumbs up only fingers towards each other. The twinkles he'd been directing towards Aggie with the Tootsie were now streaming towards Mare. "It would be a blast to work with you on this. They're sure right. You could build a water clock."

Through a tiny crack in her armor, Mare harrumphed, "After hours. I'll have a look with you."

"Sure! If you think you have any after hours. You've been working day and night."

"Okay, on a weekend, only not this Saturday, I've got to install ..."

Bobby skipped the razzing her for working Saturdays, went straight for agreeable and whatever works. "Sunday. I'll be over in the afternoon on Sunday."

Later in the day Bobby encouraged Celeste to email Mare if she wanted, but Celeste thought better of it after he left. Instead she pulled up her newfound link and shot off a note to Stuart. He would understand her 'have to tell someone.'

<< Clepsydra, Stuart. Thief of the water. Don't you like that! The water left the designated chamber through some small hole. Time was told according to where the water level lined up with marks on the inside. The word comes from the Greek, kleptein, meaning to steal. Time stole the water away. >>

Stuart knew to read in Celeste's amused laugh as he continued with her email. << Dear, once again you are the recipient of my deep appreciation. Before I could step out onto these internet avenues, I wouldn't have thought to go to the trouble of bus-to-library to research a word origin. My mind is so full these days with questions to which I can immediately find answers. Thank you, Stuart. >>

Which is how Stuart and Delaney got in on the anticipation of a water clock taking shape at Fix It, as well as the project precipitating some pretty hefty changes in the shop itself. But we'll get to that in time.

On Sunday Bobby and Mare read together from a copy of a book Richie had directed Mare to through their few rapid-fire emails back and forth. "Tuva or Bust" was an easy grab at the library. No big deal for Mare to dash to the library. Not a big run on Tuva either, at that moment nor any.

A physicist Richard Feynman and his buddy, the writer

Ralph Leighton, shared a fascination with the culture of Tuva, among its marvels the water clock. Mare was showing Bobby on page 223 "Copper bowls and chains led water down alternate paths in a slow, regular pattern ..."

"Gosh I'll bet there's a heckofa variety in design and detail ... water clocks down through the ages. Doesn't that sound like a something Celeste would have a nose for."

Bobby kind of sort of pretended he didn't hear, not wanting to get Celeste ... nor himself ... in trouble as Celeste was at that moment immersed in gathering copies of old world etchings and paintings of those very clocks.

"I'll talk to her about it," Bobby offered, in his way allowing for not needing to mention he already had.

Mare was scruffling up her hair again as she studied the pictures in Bobby's original article. "Okay Bobby, I agree, this building a water clock could be cool ... Nothing glitzy though, not even of this century."

"Art funky?"

"Not sure how that'd translate, but maybe. For sure elaborate enough that Stuart and Regoire could actually set their watches by the Fix It."

Bobby took heart. It was a good thing that the idea of a water clock made people laugh and especially so of Mare. Bobby was not about to pretend anymore. He was letting it loose. Both that he was totally drawn to Mare and to their working together on some crazy-difficult timepiece came across in his full-body grin.

Mare hesitated, "I wouldn't want to start this and not finish it."

"I get it. The design of a water clock has to grow on you." Bobby kindly left unsaid that he knew Mare needed time for 'getting close to someone again' to grow on her as well. He was okay with that. He wasn't going anywhere.

Chapter 9 ~ Assured

fr Late Latin

assēcūrāre

And there Mare was just two days later, once more eating lunch at her workbench with Bobby opposite. Aggie bounced in a seat she'd pretty much outgrown, drinking from a juice bottle and plucking cheerios out of a cup that Lorena had left for her.

Lorena and Chet were off. They'd taken the bus at the stop across the street, on out of town. Mare had sent them with directions. She had no idea that ... when they missed the campground where they were supposed to get off they would have to stay on all the way to the bay before the driver would stop. Then they had to wait out on the highway for a return bus, and once back at the campground entrance they'd have a good deal more trouble locating the reeds Mare had told them about, reeds she would show them how to cure, then weave into baskets.

Mare wasn't thinking about either project in the wings, she was eyeing Bobby who was leaned over, accepting one cheerio at a time from their little friend, closing his eyes each time she dribbled the 'o' into his mouth.

Then of a sudden Mare leapt off her stool. "Watch Aggie!" Mare tore for the door.

Out the corner of the window she'd just caught the Captain, going down. Had he walked too fast ... or who knows what ... he had definitely hit his head on the pavement. Mare fumbled to get Cap's top button undone, then took a second-thought pause to reach up behind her and rap on the window before she began mouth-to-mouth.

But Bobby was already at the door.

"Call 9-1-1."

Dialing, Bobby was at Mare's knee in a second. Juggling his cell, talking to the dispatcher, trying to assist Mare but really slowing her down. And Aggie was crying out "cahwck cahwk!" Punctuated with banging her cup on the side of the work-bench, to no avail either. Such insistence to get to her Mare. Aggie could never be mistaken for 'passive.' There she was, rocking ... and rocking ... and rocking till the bouncy seat tipped. Yet no way for a little one to compute concrete floor. She hit her head full force too, letting out such a wail that back Mare ran.

Bobby quietly changed his request for the ambulance, "Two to the hospital please."

Great gushing relief on Bobby's part, there was no blood. But a good-sized bump. The EMT thought best to get Aggie checked out. Aggie knew best to stay clinging to Mare. Marmoset tight.

On the way to the hospital the ambulance assistant wanted next of kin. Regoire had finally prevailed on Chet to get a new cell phone after Mulch's disappeared with Chet and Lorena's stolen car. Still none of them had succeeded in getting Chet and Lorena to keep the phone

With them and keep it turned on. Mare wasn't surprised when she dialed that her call went straight to voicemail. She didn't even bother.

Instead Mare called Regoire. Someone would have to sign consent papers. Luckily he answered the St. Anne phone, sparing Celeste.

Regoire put out a plate of snacks. "I'm sorry Celeste, I have a little problem," holding his temples. "I'm going to run home for a bit."

And off he went to pick up Thom who likewise excused himself from clients with "Go have coffee, see what you can work out and call me in the morning." Like a making-tracks movie, off the two sped with their godfathers' document flapping in Regoire's hand (well-notarized for just such an emergency) as they pulled into the parking lot.

On the lookout, Bobby led them at a fast pace "Through here!" into Emergency, then waited alone while the "Godfathers coming through!" found their charge.

Mare hadn't left Aggie for a second.

When the eager resident physician showed up, Regoire and Thom raised eyebrows at each other then at Mare, but no one said a word. The young doctor focused on Aggie's head, which Aggie had buried in Mare's chest. Mare did get Aggie to turn to Regoire long enough for the doctor to look closely at Aggie's pupils.

"Keep an eye on her, if she vomits more than once, get her back in here. Oh and if she's not talking normally, that might be a sign for concern."

Mare wrapped her own arms around Aggie's clutch, "lblblb-rrkr bb"

Aggie giggled right into the hiccups which had the doctor completing her diagnosis, "She's going to be just fine."

Regoire looked Mare in the eye, shifted sideways to catch Thom's near-imperceptible nod, then laid a hand on Mare's arm to stop her from getting up.

"Dr. Surer, did you say? Tremendously reassuring for

patients."

Awkward moment. Thom fumbled in trying to take back Regoire's comment, "I'm sure you've heard said numerous times."

Dr. Surer looked at Regoire, "Is there anything else?"

Again Regoire gave Mare a direct look. Something akin to a 'Sit. Stay.'

"Dr. Surer, we would like you to have a glance at Aggie's right arm, since we're here."

To her credit, Mare did not gasp.

"You see," Regoire went right on, "everything else about Aggie seems to be normal. Normal medically-attended pregnancy, easy natural birth. The one arm has simply slowed in growth during the last ... little while."

Dr. Surer pulled the rollered stool underneath her. "I'm happy to see you and all your fantastic parts, Miss Aggie. Has your mommy or daddy taught you patty cake yet?"

Not expecting a response, just easing Aggie towards further examination, Dr. Surer turned the question to Mare. "Do you know that one?"

"Oh, not very well, but I'll try."

Mare stretched her own arms out with Aggie still holding Mare's torso tight.

"Patty cake, patty crrllbl-de-blb," Mare began.

Aggie let out a whispery shriek.

Mare bent her head down and around so Aggie could see her face. "All right smartie, do it with me why don't you."

Mare swiveled Aggie to face outward, "Patty cake, patty" Aggie stretching her arms out right along with Mare, finished in unison, more or less, "crrllbl-de-blb!" Giggles and hiccups accompanying the crescendo.

The doctor filled a paper cup with water from a fresh bottle in the mini fridge and offered a drink to Aggie. While Aggie drank, the doctor held the glass with her, but also stroked Aggie's right arm and pulled the cup back to squeeze Aggie's hand, then moved the cup towards Aggie, like they were playing a game, so Aggie had to reach then bend her arm to get it back.

Dr. Surer passed the cup off to Mare and turned her attention to Regoire. "Of course you know, I am glad you asked. Very few people are aware of hemihypertrophy. Hemihyperplasia is its other name which refers to a side," she motioned up and down on her own left side, "or it could be just a portion of a side," she motioned to one, then another part of her left side, "grows more, or less. Doesn't matter which side, could be either. It's described simply as a "greater-than-normal asymmetry" and can involve any part or parts of the body, in widely varying degrees. It might just be leg hair, for instance. So far no one knows why this occurs. Studies have been slow in coming."

Dr. Surer paused. "My experience indicates that family members don't always remember what is said at a time like this so what I would like to do is have you jot down your email address and I will email you exactly what is known and what to look out for." She handed Regoire a sheet off her prescription pad. "I am not among those who believe that we need to watch watch watch," and here the doctor took a second to exchange the cup for her stethoscope, so Aggie had something to occupy her as the doctor proceeded. "You will see in my email there are real concerns. But the percentage of those who are affected is very small and there will be indicators to tip you off that you need to involve a specialist. All I want you to do at this point is the routine vigilance of any godfathers who're close by ..." She paused for breath. There was no mistaking how skilled this young doctor was in relating to families, of all sorts. "Please share this information with the parents if you will. Completely apart from the head bump, if you see any signs of your young one's stomach feeling puffy above the navel, or if she has any pain in that area, if she starts losing weight or if she is vomiting when you don't associate it with being exposed to the flu, see her doctor. And if ever hers or anyone's skin turns yellowish, that, I'm sure you know, is an emergency indicator. Aggie's coloring though ... is perfect!" Aggie showed her big grin, and the doctor took that relaxed moment to retrieve her stethoscope.

"I can tell, this is something for you to take in. You've done the right thing in asking for an opinion. I'm also going to send you a list of foods that will give her kidneys a boost. The best thing you can do for Aggie in these next five years is give her body every advantage with what she eats. Vegetables, primarily. Red peppers, garlic and onions, get her used to eating those in cooked entrees."

Mare interrupted the doctor with a burst of laughter. "Dr. Surer, you have no idea! Regoire cooks for the family and those are his staples. Plus, the parents help St. Anne's gardener in growing the best vegetables you can imagine."

Dr. Surer set aside her curiosity in what St. Anne's might

be and went right on dealing out her list like a deck of cards, "Cabbage, cauliflower."

"Check. Check."

"And fruits. Blueberries, apples, strawberries, cherries."

"Check. Check. Check, and check," Mare squeezed Aggie.

"Good. Still, I'll email you the full list. A few other items probably already in routine use." The doctor looked up, squinting as if scanning a mental chart. "Oh yes, fish!" They all only laughed so the doctor herself put a "Check!" in the air for them.

Dr. Surer attached Regoire's email address to her clipboard. "Probably take me till tomorrow to email. I am as confident as I can be at this point that we are going to see no problems developing in this child. What she has going already is simply what makes her special. I trust that you will read over the information carefully and get in touch with the family physician if you have any concerns whatsoever."

"Doctor, we can't thank you enough."

"I know. I understand. Oh, and one more thing, though it's not been documented sufficiently yet, I have read speculation that some children displaying hemi-hypertrophy have trouble identifying where pain is originating. In other words, an ankle pain on the affected side might not immediately register as coming from the ankle. So kids with hemihypertrophy may be incorrectly noted as having a high pain threshold."

Mare and Regoire exchanged concerned looks but Thom recognized that Regoire needed time to sort all this out, so he cut off further questions by thanking the doctor again for them all.

"You're welcome. Now you will excuse me, I'm sure ..." With emphasis and a wink to Regoire, "I have a full house waiting."

The three, as one, had in mind the cafeteria. Surprised that Bobby had waited all that while, Mare motioned him to join them.

While Regoire fed Aggie from a bowl of ice cream, the four adults went over the situation.

Regoire: "I take responsibility. We had an opportunity, I couldn't let that pass. If Lorena knew any of us are on the lookout for something to develop in ..." he merely smiled down to Aggie who was sitting on his lap. "That's what Lorena did not want to happen. For good or ill, I am going to share the email with you Thom, and Mare. But beyond that ..."

Bobby looked puzzled. "Are you talking about ..." he touched his own arm.

Regoire nodded ever so slightly.

Mare was relieved they were not going to talk specifics in front of Aggie. She had to ask though, to be sure they were all on the same page. "And Celeste?"

"I'll tell you," Regoire put his hand flat on the table, "I don't want Celeste to know because I want any ramifications of what we've done kept contained, just the three ..." cupping his hand and arm out to include Bobby, "the four of us. It needn't go beyond here. Not to Richie and Sadie. Not to Stuart nor Delaney. We were here, and we talked with a doctor. Period."

Later when he was by himself, Bobby would kick up his heels at being on the 'in' for a biggie at St. Anne. For now, outwardly he projected cool. "I'm good with that." Bobby didn't know anything of the particulars, and he had no need to push beyond what had already been extended to him. In time he might learn more. Till then ... he really was good.

Thom volunteered, "If at some point we do have to get medical help, I'm okay with being the Celeste liaison."

Mare, "That's good."

Regoire, "That's perfect." He put a hand on Thom's leg and as Aggie's hand followed his, Regoire moved both of theirs to a tappy dance, fingers on the table.

"crrl-bb!"

Mare missed her cue though as she was already anticipating "What about when we get back? When Lorena comes to pick her up?"

"Oh you have to tell her that much. How would she feel if she's washing Aggie's hair and comes across that …"

"You're right. I will. I'll show her the bump."

"Are you going to just avoid the hospital part?" Bobby's not sure he's tracking. "I'm just asking because I don't want to say something I shouldn't."

Regoire would later tell Thom he hadn't known Bobby had that sensitivity in him. "No, tell her. We can't keep big things from …" Regoire cut himself off as they'd been scheming to do just that. And they would, from Celeste too.

Thom, ever the one to know what to say, "Tell Lorena that a physician at the hospital looked and it's all okay and you were with Aggie the whole time."

Closed lips, thumbs up from Mare.

Regoire scooted back his chair, "So, we're set."

Mare followed suit, reaching to carry Aggie. "Wow, what an end to our lunch hour, eh Missy. Didn't expect this."

Bobby helped clear the way. "We'd better get you and Miss Aggie back before Chet and Lorena show up. Come on, you can ride in my car, sit in the back, buckle up together."

Regoire, much relieved, "This is good. Really good," ushered them along.

As they were getting into Bobby's car, the godfathers hovering, Mare realized, "Oh my gosh. The Captain."

"We'll go see how he's doing," Thom leaned in and gave Aggie a kiss on the cheek. "What's the gentleman's first name?"

Though they had little to go on other than Cap, the Fix It contingent found him, spent a good half hour more getting Cap squared away. Thom had the distinct impression that somebody was rahhing the Team.

When Mare pointed out Aggie's bump though, she tried to mitigate Lorena's concern by laying out one of her own, "Now will you and Chet carry a cell phone with you?"

But Lorena acted like she hadn't heard the question as she held Aggie's cheeks in both hands. "You look absolutely perfect to me." To Mare she added, "I think you're going to have to be in a time out."

Mare pointed to herself. "Me? You mean I'm in time out?"

"Yes. You shouldn't be letting Aggie fall."

"Okay," farewelling Aggie with a 'bllbbl'ly back and forth. "Tell me when I can come out."

Lorena hugged Aggie tight all the way out the door. Without looking back, "You can come out now!"

Lorena walked in tight circles around the gathering room, sing songing "I'm not afraid."

Celeste stayed put, eyeing. Instead of interjecting herself into *Lorena's* space though, Celeste padded down the corridor to the sunroom. Chet happened to be on his way out or in or from the looks of him hard to tell.

"Chet, is Lorena all right? Do you know?"

"She's not afraid, Celeste."

"Well good then, that's something anyway."

Chet knew. He hadn't told anyone, though not by conscious choice. He was skimming along on something like auto-pilot, 'If I forget that Dr. Lipsasch stopped us on the path, then that will help Lorena's mind with forgetting too.'

Dr. Lipsasch had caught up with them as they were walking Aggie back from the Fix It. Now that path would have a blot … for some time. For perhaps a very long time. Until the memory faded, Lorena would have to walk all the way around from Iverness, or out Harris, because the doctor had asked her nonchalantly … "How old were you when your mother died?"

"Do you have ..." the pip of a lady began. Old-fashioned as they come nowadays, buckling knee-highs, beige; Mr. Roger's cardigan, orange not red, faded and frayed so not really Mr.Roger's-like, wrapped tight around what could only be called a house dress; bobby pins more or less holding the wispy gray out of eyes hidden under piled lids. While Mare was marveling over bobby pins which she hadn't seen in years, and hoping some might fall stray, the diminutive dipped below the counter. Out of sight completely. Mare had to circle around to check that she was all right.

"Just getting this blame rock out ..." the woman stuffed her unmatched laces deep in the sides of her ...

"Reeboks?" Mare didn't mean to sound so surprised. "I'm sorry. I'm impressed, that's all. I loved my Reeboks."

"Not here 'bout no shoes. Do you have a …" The little lady recommenced her scrutiny of the shop, following a trail of anything Aggie. "… a bouncy seat? Maybe one that's got a spring sproinged, might be marked down?"

"Uhm. I'm not really … Used things yes, but appliances, and just what people've decided they didn't want after all, or ones I've come across and fixed up. You'll find a second-hand store in town, a block from …" Mare waved off the end of her directions as the woman beaded in on the play area. "Mrs. … ?"

Mare made pause as the lady veered around the workbench, hand resting on the flattened Daschund that Mare kept on hand for when she had Aggie with her. Aggie got a kick out of rolling and unrolling, the nose sticking out from one end, the tail from the other. "Mrs. ?" Mare repeated, irritated now, her one word conveying 'hey hold on!'

That snapped the woman out of her snoop. "Mrs. Lip … eh, Lickschpack …'em," the woman backed away from the dog.

Mare tried "Mrs. Lick ..." but she nearly lost it. And here this was Mare, the cagiest of St. Anne's. "Mrs. Li ..?" She had to stop again to quell the laugh.

"Limspactic ..." the woman repeated. "Lishpactemish," she tried again.

Though some, few, elderly mystery series buffs have over the years puffed themselves up out of an armchair to become certifiable P.I.s, this little lady would never. Never slip under anyone's radar, least of all Mare's. Still ...

"Nope. No jumper bumper here, Mrs. Lipsasch," she edged the cardigan'd cozener towards the door. "Have a nice life."

At least the little lady didn't try to deny being caught out.

fr Latin

pungere

'Aggie, is that a light on over at Mare's?'

Ah slumbering Aggie. Of course she wouldn't be giving what even Lorena could derive as guidance from 'asleep.' But talking to Aggie boosted Lorena's brave.

'I don't know if I can do it. What if someone's breaking into Mare's shop? I should go check for her.'

Lorena got up, turned around, crawled back under the covers. Leaned on an elbow. Looked out the window. 'It's a light. I have to be sure no one's breaking in.'

Lorena stood up, crossed to the door, stepped into the hall, then turned back to bed. Seven times Lorena turned to bed. It seemed like seven. Felt rather like a seven, going out turning back.

On the eighth standing she found herself tiptoeing along the pathway beyond the arched bridge. Lorena kept her head up, breathed in and out. But opposite to how she'd been taught, that got her heart to racing really fast so she switched, took a gulp and held her breath. But that made inching more like centimetering. Through the dark. Creepers tendriling out on the path now. One on her foot. One tickling her other ankle. The foot one was circling up around her calf ...

Lorena lurched!

"Chet! Chet, you can't sleep over! I have dreams when you sleep over."

"I didn't know, 'rena. I thought you wanted me to protect you. You and Aggie." Chet reached to the baby bed, barely touching Aggie's arm.

Lorena stretched her leg over Chet's.

"Do you want me to go home now?"

Lorena linked her leg around Chet's.

"'rena, it's dark out."

"No, you can stay, Chet. I'll stay awake."

"That'll work, 'rennie. Do you want to play Crazy Eights?"

"Chet, it's dark out."

No one had told Lorena outright about the doctor coming to Fix It … nor about the doctor's mother poking about. No one had seen Claire either yet, but yes, Claire was on the prowl. Flick to movie adaptation, dip into bass notes, minor key it and the week following the Mrs.'s visit, you'll be in step for Mare's "What the ___!" spotting Claire.

Even without any updates from others, Lorena had for some time been switched over to her own instinctive stuff-baby-under-wing mode. Inevitably, eventually Aggie's tractability waned. Mighty uncomfortable, being lumped in a back-carrier all day. Lorena understood that much. Not knowing what else to do, she returned to letting Aggie run free, which flipped her inner switch at 'back to normal.'

The effects didn't stop though.

"Chet, I need a hug."

"'rena, I don't think we should have another baby."

"Chetty! I don't mean that! I just need a hug."

Chet stepped up, hugged Lorena like there's no end in the world, Aggie in on it too.

"Oh Chetty. You're the best."

"'rennie. I can give hugs any time you want."

She dove into a hug again, separating only after the longest closest, matched-up hug.

"Good one, Chet. Me too. I like ... that."

Mulch excused himself even before he came in, as he held the door open and slipped off his boots. Stepping into the sunroom and up to Celeste's desk, "I's jus' wondering if you'd noticed, do Miss Lorena 'ppear 'xactly herself these days, tuh you?"

"What have you noticed? Can you give me an example?

"Is likes, she'll be out in the garden. I thinks she's watchin' the l'il one an' next thing I knows, Miss Ags there'll be inside the chicken coop, stirrin' up them chickens an 'rena won't even knows. As ifs she's off in 'er head some'here."

"I can picture that perfectly, Mulch. I understand what you're asking now. Now that you have me thinking along those lines, I expect you may be right. It does seem Lorena is more disconnected than she has been. More like she used to ... I appreciate you bringing this to my attention. I'll speak with Regoire."

On his way out Mulch sideways'd mid-shuffle, "Tha Thom mi'ht have sum idears. He's a good one for 'elp."

"Definitely. Very good. Thank you. I'll bring Thom in on the discussion. Yes."

"You'll let me know if I should be doin' sumpin diff'rent with l'il Miss Aggie?"

"I will. Thank you, Mulch."

Mulch tipped the brim of his hat which he had donned prematurely, his 'Welcome, m'am' slipped onto the step as he pulled on his boots.

That very afternoon, Lorena wandered into the gathering room, then minutes later idled out. There was nothing unusual in her leaving her dust cloth on a window ledge, as Celeste explained it to Regoire later, but setting about to dust and not dusting a spec certainly wasn't in line with her training. And not like Lorena.

Neither Celeste nor Regoire came up with anything. Only a pact between them to keep an eye on her ... and Aggie, of course. But that was nothing more than they'd been doing all along.

Now this may sound like Celeste was remiss, but in her mind there did not seem to be anything she could do ... except maybe make progress on identifying the cause for Lorena's reverting to her old ways. Thom had talked the

Lipsasches into a cease and desist in exchange for some off-site consultation, prompting Regoire to come clean to Celeste about Lipsasch's return.

"What do you mean that doctor's been around and now he's not. Why didn't you tell me?"

"We thought …"

"Regoire, are you trying to make me furious with you? Why was I kept in the dark? When did you intend to let me in on this risk to the child and her baby?"

Regoire's look could convey 'that's exactly why' with a hint of 'you don't stay rational at times like this' more pointedly than anyone Celeste had ever known.

"You say Thom is handling this, that he'll get the doctor to leave Lorena alone?"

"That's what we believe, yes. Thom's had some assurances already."

And Regoire believed her when she sighed "All right then."

So no one suspected that Celeste was up to anything in particular at her computer. Celeste couldn't get it out of her head though, 'the more we can learn the better' as she was far from satisfied that 'the doctor' and his sympathizers would actually leave them be. Lorena had regressed, there was no doubt in Celeste's mind about that. She'd try to keep watch, be much more attentive. But she decided if no one else was going to get to the bottom of this ridiculous threat, whatever the link was between Lorena and Claire and that 'blame doctor' she would have to figure it out herself.

Soon Celeste had a pile-up on her Notepad. Yes, Celeste loved the many play-tools on computer and web. She intended to share with Stuart when he came by with deliveries, as she knew he too thought there was more behind the scenes than anyone had been letting on.

Celeste began with Dr. I.M. Lipsasch's education. Though she couldn't figure out if there was a way to access transcripts online, she accepted that he had received degrees in his name. However any indication of his status through med school appeared completely out of reach as the doctor's alma mater had gone belly up. And regarding his career, other than his current practice which was, as young people would say, sketchy, she found nothing about his professional history. Celeste wondered if Dr. Lipsasch had employed researchers. Assistants would have the inside eye.

'Stuart,' Celeste clicked in her phone Contacts. "Stuart, I'm ready for a Facebook account."

"Yes, Celeste, I'm sure you are," he answered through his headset as he was on his way to another client. "Why don't you see if you can walk yourself through it. You'll need to set up a personal ID and Home page. If you get stuck I'll be by this afternoon."

She did. And she didn't. By the time Stuart was off work, Celeste had Friended twenty people on her way to one hundred.

"I'm impressed. … No. Actually I thought you would be

118

able to get yourself on Facebook. How do you like it?"

She pointed to her Facebook Friends, "I'm going to have an Instagram account as well."

"What for, Celeste?"

"I like to see what our friends are up to," she hedged. "Is there a problem with that? Something I don't know?" she challenged.

"No, not at all. I'll be interested to hear how you find Instagram."

Celeste grinned at being on the forefront with social media. Or at least ahead of Stuart this once.

"I will, Stuart dear. I will." Celeste was already heading back into her laptop. "Stuart," she said, not looking at him, "you know there are thousands of things I don't know how to do on the computer, thoroughfares I won't even know exist until I happen onto them. That seems like the way of this cyber world. I may have never known about Pinterest until I was drawn there ... a new Friend had posted 'a Pin' ... so I found directions how to Pin too," Celeste's stretched as wide as the smiley-faced animals she'd just clicked to on Pinterest. "But Finsta, we can leave that to the teens."

"Finsta?"

"Oh don't worry dear, you're much too old for Finsta."

"Stuart so wished for a Delaney or Mare as he squelched a double-take for lack of receiver. Instead he replaced with predictable, yet more than ever unnecessarily sensible response, "Well you're doing remarkably well. Miles beyond most of my students."

Celeste shot him a look, reminding him she was not.

"Yes, yes, you're right. Self-taught all the way!"

"And now if you'll excuse me, I've got some work to do. ..." Then, half with him still, "How is Delaney ... how are you two doing?" She reached to pat Stuart's arm, only caught his cuff as she was, as they say, glued to the screen.

"I'll go now, Celeste. You're busy. Delaney and I are doing just fine." He gave her shoulders a hug, offered, "If you're ever of a mind to come out, we'd like to treat you ..."

"Oh why don't you and Delaney come here, Stuart. It makes Regoire so happy to cook for a group."

"As you wish, Celeste." He held still ... There was no way Celeste would recognize Westley from "The Princess Bride." Stuart screwed up his face remembering a time when Celeste might at least ask if he was quoting a movie. When no specific invitation was forthcoming, Stuart made his way out, confiding the oddity to Delaney later. At the front door though he turned and went back down the hallway to the sunroom, but Celeste was already deep into Facebook, scanning once again through not only Dr. Lipsasch's handful of Friends, but giving another look at Claire's as well. So Stuart left.

When Regoire stepped up alongside her to offer a glass of water sprigged with chocolate mint and a demi plate of sliced Asian pear, Celeste merely gave a 'hmm,' nodded sideways without looking up. Brushing off the slight, Regoire let her be.

'Oh Lora, you would have loved this search engine!'

Lora might've countered 'who do you think is doing the steering, Celeste,' but Celeste wasn't picking up on Lora's vibes any better than those from her dears in the flesh.

Celeste did zero in on where Claire was "From …" though, then traveled through search bar to a Portland suburb, a crossroads only really, one she'd never heard of outside Lake Oswego.

"Hazelia! Now we're getting somewhere."

Celeste's fingers click clicked into several dead ends.

"Regoire!"

Regoire eyed her out the pass-through. He didn't always come running.

"What does Hazelia sound like to you?"

122

"It sounds ... I have no idea. Why, Celeste? What are you after now?"

"It looks like Claire grew up in Hazelia."

"Celeste!" Regoire turned back to his work. He'd long ago stopped encouraging Celeste's wild speculations. Regoire didn't have a degree in clinical psychology either, but he knew better than to practice without one.

"Hear me out now, Regoire. If Claire grew up in Hazelia, that's farther afield than Lake Oswego but close enough to get a constant whiff of what she didn't have from out in farm country. That could explain Claire's snipey on-the-outside wanting-in demeanor, couldn't it."

Regoire didn't answer. Celeste's hadn't really posed a question anyway.

And Celeste didn't notice as she was already on the trail for a link between anyone Lipsasch and Hazelia. Hopping in and out of chat groups. Cruising to see if Dr. Lipsasch had drawn any recommendations or even associates through his Linkedin account … any route to Hazelia.

'Nothing, Lora. I suppose you're able to keep discouragement at bay, aren't you my free-spirit friend. Any idea where we should look next?'

Whether Lora was actually responding or not, debatable of course. Nevertheless at that moment Celeste's right calf cramped up, so much so that she had to scoot away from the computer.

'I'm going to lie down,' she whispered toward Regoire as she massaged her leg enough to be able to stand.

"If you want a walk, I'm about done here and I can go with you out to the garden."

Celeste was still so in her head, she didn't even respond. And later after her hour and a half nap she was right back at it.

"Ah ha! That's it. Even the Hazelia Literary and Debating Society had lost momentum a full generation before Claire came on the scene. I'll bet you anything, Claire's being excluded from the cultural refinements of the privileged Lake Oswegoites set that chip on her shoulder with powerful need to make some kind of mark in the world."

But no one was listening to Celeste's deductions.

fr Latin
dēsignāre

It was Thom. Thom who had no interest in searching on the internet about real people with whom, if he got the chance, he could converse directly. It was Thom, after all, who knew how to listen. He listened to Dr. Lipsasch. Murley. Murley Lipsasch. And, with the exception of Claire who had other senses in play which made it hard for her to hear clearly, no one had listened to Murley, ever.

Only barely into their meeting, with Dr. Lipsasch coming to Thom's office, Thom suggested they walk instead. "There's a mini lake. Let's go from here. You'll like it."

There was nothing calculating in Thom either. Thom was just ... being Thom. On route to the small arboretum not far from Thom's office, they got a rhythm going, which in a wordless way created comfortable rapport between the two gentlemen. And that opened the gates as if Thom had been leading with questions from the start.

"Thom, please believe me, I have not wanted to upset anyone at St. Anne's."

"I do, Murley. I understand how things can get blown out of proportion."

"I can't tell you how good this feels to be able to confide in you."

Simply, "I'm glad. You can."

"That word proportion. There's this portion I've known that I couldn't let known, so we've had misunderstanding on top of misunderstanding. I was trying to protect someone, and in the process others needed protection ... from me," Murley choked.

"Whenever you want ... it's okay."

Murley pulled out a handkerchief and blew his nose. "First, is it possible for you to see me as separate from Claire? To put it bluntly, I played Claire, Thom. I'm not proud of it, but that's the way it was."

"Oh?"

"Yes, I knew that she worked for Celeste on occasion and I knew … well, it didn't take anything to ascertain that Claire was in great want of a man."

Thom raised an eyebrow.

"I'm sorry to have to admit it, but that's how important getting close to Lorena had become to me. I … prepped Claire."

Thom looked Murley square in the face.

"Yes, I seduced that poor woman … although after doing so I can tell you there's no 'poor' about Claire. I'd told Claire that cock 'n bull story about my study because, well, there were benefits in our friendship. You see, she had designs of her own … Just never mind all that. Claire really had no part of this what I want to tell you."

"I can accept what you're saying," offered Thom, as noncommittally as he could muster.

"My whole purpose in involving Lorena in a mock study ..."

Though he usually did better, in this instance Thom couldn't help sucking in his breath.

"Yes, I'm sorry to say, it was all a ruse. We're in confidence here as you promised, correct?"

"Go on." Thom kept them walking.

Murley clapped a hand on Thom's sleeve pulling them both to a stop. "The reason I wanted to get close to Lorena ... I wanted to find out if my brother was Lorena's father. He wasn't sure and it was tearing him apart. I could've lived with that, but our mother ..."

"Mmm," surprised but not showing it, "I understand."

"I'd planned to get a DNA sample when Claire brought Lorena a second time, but then there was that terrible situation with her reaction to my placebo."

"I'd hardly call it a 'situation.'" Thom, even pro that he

was, fell a step or so behind in processing Murley's bombshell.

"You have every right to be peeved. Anyway, Mother landed a pacifier, brought it home from the shop in her purse and we had that tested. I compared it to our family's DNA. My brother was not involved."

Now if Regoire had been present to this unfolding, or heaven forbid, Celeste, heads would have rolled. But it was Thom. Thom who responded with a simple purposeful monotone, "I'm relieved."

"You understand, I wanted you to know. Now that we have it my brother is not Lorena's father, we're satisfied. And you won't see us anymore."

"I'm sorry, Murley, ordinarily this kind of conversation stays confidential. What a dilemma you've placed me in though. I'll give you some time to prove what you say, staying out of our lives, I mean. Claire too! But eventually I am going to share this information with our St. Anne family. They need to know, the overhanging menace has lifted. And they all deserve to know the why behind what you brought to St. Anne."

"You do what you have to do. I'm just glad this is behind us."

Thom was thinking 'You have no idea how far from "behind us" this is for our Lorena.' But he had his wits back enough to hold his tongue. The last thing they needed was for Murley to be drawn back in.

For Claire, the 'behind her' would no doubt take time. After the reveal to Thom, Dr. Lipsasch could have chosen to pass forward Thom's consideration and let Claire down, easily. But it took an acerbic twist from Murley to even be able to disengage himself. In a huff Claire did move up the coast, believing a person could actually start over. At least her association with St. Anne's was over for good.

While Thom edged beyond his initial 'stunned,' looking for when and how he could let his dear friends at St. Anne in on what he'd found out, Celeste carried on in the dark. She still didn't even know Dr. Lipsasch's given name, finding in all her searches only his first and middle initials. And Thom had no idea, though he might have guessed, how Celeste could not leave it alone. Morning and night she was at her desk in the sunroom, one more avenue, one last turn, hoping she might latch onto the source of Dr. Lipsach's obsession with Lorena and Aggie.

'Celeste, you're rubbing your eyes. Why don't you take a break.' Regoire, Stuart, Mare all tried to get through to her. Everyone except Lorena who was barely keeping herself together.

Even without any direct input from Lora, Celeste had it in her bones there was some story in the doctor's past. Doggedly she kept nose to ground. A newspaper article might tell her. Had Lipsasch's mother remarried? Did he go by a different last name as a child? Had he had a sibling who embarrassed the family? Had the doctor committed some horrific lapse of judgment, or had his folks? Or was it something more benign? A professor in college who sparked an interest that had Dr. Lipsasch wanting to prove his worth?

Or, or, or, she might hit upon it down a different alley. Who were Lipsasch's current Friends? What associations did any of them have to Claire? To developmental disorders? Even to child development? Celeste made lists on her lists trying to find overlaps. For someone who'd never watched afternoon soaps, Celeste trailed a storyline that could've kept the drama on air for seasons. If she could just find the thread, she envisioned threatening the doctor with a public unraveling that would force him to desist.

Certainly, if Thom had seen firsthand how Lorena was slipping away, he would've found the right words and way to put a stop to her pain. Truthfully Celeste was hardly aware of Lorena day to day as they both stayed stuck in the slippage.

Celeste wasn't alone in being confounded by the drama. Too soon it turned out that Lorena's needing more hugs was more hugs than Chet could provide. But how would Chet have known 'rena would be pulling in for fill-ups, one after another.

When Lorena would sidle up to Chet, Aggie in tow, Chet would just as likely drop to his knees to walk his fingers over Aggie's feet as stand to give Lorena her hug. Aggie would laugh of course, but laughter flitted, without assuaging Lorena. Sometimes, drained Chet pretended he hadn't seen them coming, or that he heard Mulch calling him away. So increasingly Lorena withdrew, her visage vacant, masked the same as after the earthquake, those moments everyone realized Stuart might be in the tunnel.

At least Lorena had the benefit of having relocated her old emotional crawlspace.

Pre-Aggie, Celeste surely would have taken charge, guided Lorena, or as she'd done after the quake, directed Chet. And coming from Celeste, Chet would have done whatever Celeste asked. Lorena's 'new momma' assertiveness through those first many months had curbed Celeste's stepping in at every turn.

Though renewed care would have been justified, Celeste really wanted to avoid stirring up what Regoire saw as her meddling. So she kept on her circuitous route, doubling down on the cyber search. One more hour and she thought she would have it.

Then ... Regoire pulled in from his trip to the Fish Market one afternoon, found Aggie on his back doorstep. Yes, on the outside of the garden enclosure, stacking twigs all by herself. It took everything in Regoire to breathe into calm as he gathered Aggie up in his arms.

He had her peek in his fish-smelly bag, talking soothingly about what was for dinner. And he jibbered to her about whatever he could think of other than 'What are you doing out here?' as he walked them the direct path to the front door hoping he'd come upon Lorena nearby. He came upon Lorena all right, though, sound asleep in her suite.

Regoire enticed Aggie down the hall with promise of muffin and milk. Once they had his purchases put away in the back fridge, and he'd gotten Aggie set up in the sunroom, Regoire went to the outlet by Celeste's desk ... and pulled the plug. Just like that. No word of warning. Perhaps he wasn't fully aware that her laptop would be blinking when she next booted up: Incorrectly Shut Down. At that moment he would not have cared. Regoire was holding back fury. Even if he didn't know the thing about computers, he knew what that blame thing was doing to St. Anne's.

"What? Regoire! You've just made me lose a propitious link."

"As you can see I am checking my response," Regoire dialed his emotions down at least ten notches, "because as you can see," he repeated, "we are not alone."

"Aggie, I didn't hear you come in."

"And neither did anyone else, Celeste. This day will not close until you and I have had a proper talk. Until later," he stressed, making it clear the two of them would wait to talk in private, "please, Aggie is with us," again putting emphasis on the 'us' so Celeste would take into account Lorena's absence. "Likely she's going to need a trip to the bathroom. Help her with that at least ... please," weighted with nothing near pleasant.

Well before dinner Lorena woke, located Aggie and went right on without a bit of acknowledgment that she had checked out. Regoire bided his time, made up an excuse about a prep for tomorrow's meal planning so he would still be there till Lorena got Aggie to bed.

In the interim, Celeste found herself free to make sure her computer was okay, ringing Stuart to see if she needed to do anything in particular when turning it back on. She started to ask Stuart 'what's gotten into Regoire' but stopped herself. Ordinarily a question like that was well within Stuart and Celeste's purview, but Celeste's ultimate loyalty was after all ever with Regoire. So until he told her what he was upset about, she held her tongue.

Stuart advised that an occasional disconnect would probably not do any damage. Even so, he gave her instructions for resetting the pram. Whenever attempting something new, Celeste had to block out everything else. So it didn't help matters when Regoire happened to find her head into her computer when he wanted to reconnect.

"Celeste, that is it! I have just served you sole picatta, the lemon sauce with capers the way you like it best. I'll bet you didn't even see the slathering of shiitake mushrooms I added. Granted it's a lightweight entrée but I had a few things on my mind." Right there he wanted her to ask what. When she didn't he just kept on, record stuck. "It was cooked in one of our better white wines, creamed peas and baby onions, yes, from the garden, my own country bread. You hardly tasted any of it, did you? Perhaps you would have preferred I'd spent hours on an elusive Bouillabaisse instead."

Regoire certainly had her attention. She was thinking, 'This isn't like you, sweet friend. Why, I've never heard you complain about time or effort in a meal. Ever.' But she kept her mouth shut. Her eyes welled though as he went on. For the moment, Regoire lost track of what he'd wanted to discuss. Utterly derailed, "What's the use! Would you notice the slivered fennel these days ... or ... Celeste, here's a good example, ordinarily you'd be intrigued that the saffron I've been using this month comes from a new rebuilding group in Afghanistan."

She was trying to follow him. Really she was. When she still came up speechless, he summed up, repeating "Why bother!" He meant with trying to explain. He was halfway to his cuisine when he pivoted, "And that's what everyone in St. Anne's has thought, though no one has said so to you." Regoire turned on his heel a second time, back to safe haven.

Celeste would ordinarily react to his challenge, if nothing else than to her preferences in eating. Always they were on the same page completely when it came to St. Anne's meals. But in this, however she looked at it, she had no leg to stand on. His words hit her hard because they rang so true. Never had she not appreciated Regoire's cooking. If Regoire hadn't named the dish, she would not have been able to tell Stuart what they'd had for dinner. And Stuart ... when had she last had a friendly person-to-person conversation with Stuart, discussing favorite sauces or desserts? When had she last listened to Delaney or Mare either? Recognition. Aghast, she got up, made her way across the sunroom more slowly than usual. And further out of the ordinary, she knocked first before stepping into la cuisine.

"How long has this been going on, Regoire? Heavens, what have I missed!"

"That's what I'm telling you, Celeste. You've darn near missed ... I can't even talk right ... Mulch."

"Mulch?"

"Mulch has been in to see me 'darn near evry day' so much that I'm talking like him. If I'd listened to Mulch weeks back."

"You mean he's upset ... Oh. I know. He came to me a while ago too. Remember, we talked ... didn't we?"

Regoire looked her in the eye until she had to turn away. Regoire called Thom. While Celeste was standing right there. Thom came over immediately.

Celeste had gone back to the sunroom. She had taken her laptop to the table with her, to close down. Her mind was muddled but she tuned as best she could to Thom and Regoire who came in to join her.

"Celeste, we have something to tell you about Lorena," Thom began.

"But first," Regoire put a hand out to Thom, then faced Celeste, "You should know why I went out of my mind tonight."

With his "Aggie being where she could've wandered off" Celeste blanched.

"I was just inside here. And I had no … Regoire, you have to know, I've only been on the computer these days to find out what's going on with that horrid doctor … so I could get Lorena back."

"There's something that's going to help, Celeste."

And Thom went right to filling Celeste in on what his time with the doctor had yielded.

"I can scarcely believe it. Thom, I got nowhere near uncovering what you did. And that's all it was? Paternity?" Celeste pushed her computer, away from her as far as she could. "That's it then. It's done. We don't need any of what I tracked down."

Thom looked to Regoire.

"What about Claire?" Celeste thought that's what the two of them were about to bring up.

"No, there's nothing about Claire. She was a peripheral player. Never a part of the main concern. Murley will take care of Claire."

"Murley?"

"That's the doctor's first name."

Celeste laughed outright, "He didn't want it known!"

Regoire and Thom conferred again with a look.

"I'm so sorry. I am so sorry. What can I do?" Celeste believed they were back to Aggie's care, which in a way they were. She was picking up on that correctly.

"What you've always done, Celeste. Be here. Listen. Get Lorena talking to you again. But you'll have to give that time to redevelop. In the long run, your imperturbability," Celeste couldn't help but smile as Thom nearly missed a syllable, "is going to matter most. Yes, and give her a hand with Aggie if she seems to need it ... if you're able."

"That's going to help Chet too," Regoire added, Thom not quite sure why.

Thom shook his head, an involuntary clearing space.

Finally he was getting to it. For days he'd been trying to figure out what of all this he could tell Lorena. How, if even possible, could he link the dots for her? But instead Thom had hit on the question he was about to ask Celeste.

"How old was Lorena when Lora left?"

"You mean when she left … ?" Celeste scooted sideways closer to the window, scanning to be sure none of her little family had slipped into the garden, never mind the unlikelihood in the dark. Stalling.

Eyes on her, Thom and Regoire wouldn't let her escape.

"Thom, for heavens sake."

"Just watch her, Celeste. See what you think in that light."

Thrice stunned in one day, Celeste didn't know what she thought about anything.

"Delaney," she began speaking before her dial connected. Celeste had spent the day wondering, watching Lorena and Aggie as she could. Talking to Aggie some little bit. Wanting to touch Lorena. 'Give it time' though? She just wasn't able.

"Delaney, might I have a word with you and Stuart, please. ... No, no hurry ... Well, if possible tomorrow, around your work schedules."

They came the following day together during lunch hour. Lorena let them in but didn't stay to talk.

"What is it, Celeste?" both asked, seemingly unaware of how their voices were braiding up.

"Can you tell me, have you noticed anything in Lorena?"

Celeste looked from one to the other, making a mental note that she might do well to meet with these two separately more, as she used to. Celeste's question turned Delaney and Stuart to each other further, each wondering who would go first and how much they would say. Celeste saw, as a couple they seemed to have talked about this together just as Regoire and Thom had.

"I've been concerned, Celeste." But then Stuart opened his hand to Delaney.

"I haven't been with Lorena much lately," Delaney took up, "but I could see what Stuart has noticed by how Lorena answered the door."

"She hardly did. Like she's behind a veil."

"That's it exactly," Delaney continued. "It's subtle, but Lorena doesn't seem 'there' ... not 'here' the way she was through pregnancy and those first mothering months."

They talked it around but in the end there wasn't much more to say.

The next day during Aggie's nap Celeste did what she'd always done. She drew Lorena aside. And she did what she'd been trying not to do since Aggie was born ... Oh, her effort to the contrary had been out of deference to Regoire and Thom all right, mostly for Regoire who was sure Celeste interfered too much.

In part he'd certainly been right. Celeste recognized the many small ways she could do better at encouraging Lorena's independent adulthood. Referring to Lorena as a child had needed to change, yes. But in taking Regoire's input she had swung too far. Celeste was actually the only one who had ever truly understood Lorena's innate fluctuating abilities. It was time Celeste get them back to comfort. As if pulling on old slippers she'd misplaced for too long and handing Lorena hers, Celeste began.

"Lorena, look at me."

Celeste waited until she did.

"This is important sweetheart. I've been thinking."

Celeste held till she had Lorena's full attention.

"Darling, just because your mother died when you were a wee girl, doesn't mean you will die during Aggie's youngest years too. Why Lorena, you could live to be 110."

Lorena sat up straighter, eyes beading in, to inward. Lorena blinked. Big.

She stood up. Turned and twisted her lower body parts.
Twirled her wrists, loosening binds.
Squeezed her hands and tugged at her fingers.
Plopped back down, blinked again slowly.

Then as if she had replaced the indoor footwear with a favorite weather-worn coat herself, Lorena walked right out of the house. But yes, you're following correctly, coatless. And she didn't even check that Celeste knew to take charge of Aggie.

"What now!" Celeste breathed.

Celeste lifted an energized Aggie onto her lap a full hour later, at her desk in the sunroom. Aggie beat on the top of Celeste's laptop with her little open palms. But Celeste was quick to set her straight.

"No little one, we are done with the computer for a while. I have to stay with St. Anne better than I have been."

Aggie surprised Celeste, craned, planted very wet kiss on Celeste's neck.

That minute, there came Lorena, charging in the front door, shivering. Door slipped and slammed in the wind which shook the shelves that held Aggie's figurines, plenty safe though in their little glass boxes.

"Celeste! I'm home!"

"Well thank goodness for that."

Lorena stood in the doorway to the sunroom.

"Ready for tea?" Regoire had heard and could be heard preparing.

"Come here, darling. Let's have a hug first."

Aggie did the most of it, sandwiched as she was, but at least Lorena and Celeste were touching in, and just maybe, pointing in the same direction again.

And 'what?' you say? Of course distanced-selves don't usually 'come home' quite that easily. But you have to admit, it's entirely like Lorena to see something from a new angle and of a sudden be able to make the 180 ... in yes, even in under an hour. Lorena might churn and withdraw for weeks, but once things cleared, clear for her, she simply let life have her and sailed on.

That's how it happened. That's how the all that was Lorena returned, after Thom and Regoire had their talk with Celeste. And Celeste in turn had hers with Lorena. But then Lorena had needed one more thing. Her charging out the door wasn't leaving at all. She had marched over to Mulch's to find Chet. To give him a hug. And ... to 'make a pact' she called it. She needed a pact that one or the other of them would absolutely live to 103. She didn't care who and she didn't care how. Chet was fine that.

With their plan set, and with Dr. Lipsasch no longer lurking about ... neither parent had seen him for days ...

Lorena was relieved of her fear for Aggie. That's all it took for Lorena to land on her middle ground again.

Regoire didn't care about absolutes either. He could see enough from the smiles at table to on the spot propose a party.

"Lorena, how would you and Aggie like to help me make a monstrous batch of codfish nuggets for dinner tonight. We'll have chips and coleslaw and if we get a move on we could even come up with some bread sticks. You like bread sticks, right there little one?"

"Crck-crrckkgabrr!"

"I don't know about that," Regoire squeezed Aggie's upraised fingers.

"But Mare will. Can we invite Mare, Regoire?"

"Let's get the whole lot of them, what do you say, Celeste? Will you do the phoning to see who can make it on such short notice? Lorena and I have a meal to prepare! ... All the regulars, and you've got Bobby's number, right?"

"Bobby?"

"Yes, he's definitely on our list."

'I missed that too?' Celeste wondered not for the last time what all had gone on without her knowing.

"Yes, I can reach Bobby ... I think."

"Call Thom first. He'll know."

Funny how we shake our heads. It was Celeste's turn, to let things go. And what relief came welling. No one blaming her. Regoire feeling good again. Lorena in la cuisine!

'Thom and Bobby?' though. She couldn't help marveling at all that had gone on, without her being aware. But she could do this ... she would let go of wanting full updates on what she didn't know. And if she had any questions along the way, she'd keep quiet enough for Regoire not to hear. Today anyway. Celeste was well aware she'd thrown plenty enough monkey wrenches for a lifetime.

"And Celeste, sorry, but we are not going to have time to prepare mushy peas."

"Ha!"

Like getting one of those really good hugs from an old friend, Celeste let it in. Was Regoire really in his groove? Lorena had laughed too, not knowing the joke. No one but the oldest of friends would know how much Celeste did not care for the Brit's mushy peas, ever, no matter how much a cook might want to keep them on a traditional menu. To have Regoire teasing her. Could she really hope they had made it back?

"But I'll make the cucumber slivers you like," both their smiles broadened, remembering a time when Celeste was first tasting Regoire's style of cooking before he even came to St. Anne. "With mini ramekins of sautéed kale," he went serious again, "for good standing." Then, "And for dessert ... we'll cook up something, won't we my sweets."

Celeste started with Thom. It didn't take her long to find out, the others were on their way to being gathered already.

Delaney's cell rang. "I want to get this."

"O'course." Mare motioned Bobby to the sketch Delaney had been showing her.

"Hi Stuart."

"Hi Del. You know my last stop? They're going away and forgot to tell me, so they didn't need anything this afternoon. I'm done early. Where are you?"

"Bobby and I are over at Mare's. Come over. We could use your take on some style ..." Delaney shrugged, grinned to Mare.

"I'll be right over."

Since Mare was laughing at her, "I had to give him something. Stuart doesn't possess much construction know-how."

"Heck, I'd like his ideas once we get to the water clock!"

Bobby leaned his upper body towards Mare, lining up face to face. "So, we're doing it, eh?"

"If. If we do it."

Delaney shot Mare a girls' grin from behind Bobby. She knew what Mare was up to. Mare wasn't about to make it too easy on Bobby. Delaney's look said it 'You're bad!' in that good understanding each other way.

And Bobby? He could see Delaney's reflection in the window, knew exactly what the two women were doing, but had no need whatsoever to let on he knew.

When they heard Stuart calling from inside the shop, Mare yelled "We're out here!" Disinclined to traipse through Mare's private space, Stuart retraced his steps, worked his way around the building to the outside north wall.

"So, this is exciting. What are you all cooking up?"

They gave him the low down, Mare's need for an area where work of a private nature could be set out undisrupted during the course of a fix-it day.

"Mare, I think you short-change Celeste. She'll understand completely."

"Oh I'm sure she'll be amenable. I just want to present it right. It's not just an addition for the water clock. It'll be for whatever projects any of us want to work on."

Bobby bobbed his eyebrows at Stuart with an all-too 'dontcha just love this' grin, then corrected himself to Mare, "Now don't worry, there'll be no getting ahead of myself," at which Mare rolled her eyes to Delaney.

"Let's get down some dimensions so we know what we're taking to Celeste."

"This gets a little tricky since I don't own the building. Economical as possible though."

"I always do for Celeste even if she doesn't need it."

"Well, since I'm paying for this addition ..."

"Right, got it."

Bobby held the tape end for Delaney to measure off, including what they'd need for natural light.

"What do you think about skylights rather than windows?

We can build them ourselves. Believe me I learned the hard way how to make a skylight that won't leak, even on this coast."

"And I know I said low cost," Mare, unthinking, clutched Bobby's arm, excited at some image of another project they might tackle together. Instantly she shook herself, let go and grabbed Stuart instead. "Stuart, what do you think about raising the height in the addition? An extra six feet might come in handy."

That would mean redesigning a roofline to fit with the Fix It's. Nothing Delaney couldn't handle easily though. She entered Mare's decisions, spare as they were, on her BuildCalc app. They'd have a figure.

It was about then Celeste's first call came through so they pressed ahead to get an initial plan at least, in time for dinner.

fr Old North French
cachier

Lorena was still in la cuisine with Regoire, Lorena singing some words-changing round.

Aggie was lying on her back in the sunroom, trying to mimic her daddy's leg lifts.

"Would you like me to help you pick up those sticks? Aren't those uncomfortable underneath you?"

"No that's okay, Celeste," Chet rolled in silliness, pretty disconnected from the crunch crunch.

"Crnk Crnk" Aggie giggled, in synch with her Daddy, and equally detached from having been the bringer-in-er of sticks.

As they waited ... Stuart and Delaney arriving, then Thom from the other direction, Bobby, lastly Mare ... Chet's nose twitched towards la cuisine. That first batch

of fish starting to cook got his mouth watering seafood and that hopped his mind to other things sea. It took getting to, but he and Mare had finally carted off the last of the shrimp tanks. So when Chet began an impromptu game for picking up those sticks, adding a new word with each one, it was only natural what popped out:
"Shrimp
farm
flarm
sharm
shrimp farm," repeated with variants as one would expect. Aggie chimed in, shrieks turning to hiccups.

But Mulch prodded, then followed Chet's bobbing to the garden, Chet clicking sticks to the beat in his head, then flipping one at a time in rhythm in the direction of the compost. Perspectives are. Chet could tell from Mulch's scowl as they left the sunroom that his entertaining Aggie with shrimp farm ditties was about to devolve into serious conversation. Of course Mulch saw it exactly t'other way round.

"Yous have tuh study up. You can't go 'bout sumpin like this halfways.

"What?" knowing very well what.

"You knows what I'm talkin' 'bout."

"I am study ... er, Lorena is. ... Lorena was. We haven't talked shrimpsies ... you know ... while Lorena ... Stuart, he found us the order place though so we're all set ... when 'rena says 'ready.'"

"There's a lot more goes into 'n operation then ordering them baby shrimp. You know what I think. I think you should ask that Celeste of yours. She be just sittin' in there most days, knowin' she should stay out of the Fix It and not knowin' what to do with'erself ih'stead."

"Celeste." Chet considered for half a second. "No, Mulch, 'rena would have told me if Celeste knows about shrimp."

Chet loved Celeste no end, but he had that belief about the upper age brackets. Excluding Mulch, of course. Mulch worked physically all day every day so Chet didn't consider Mulch expired. But Celeste? What did she do? And what could she know about stuff like shrimp?

"Look at 'er in there, look right there she is. You goes in there and asks her if she kin open up that computer o' hers, meybe t'morrow. Just tell 'er what you want tuh know. It's not as she knows it, it's as she kin find it for ya."

Chet was giving a little consideration to whether he cared. It was Lorena who had gotten wind of the shrimp tanks in the first place. And soon after it was Lorena pressed 'Mare to tell her what she knew about shrimp farms, then 'rena went straight to Chet, convinced him that it was their destiny to grow shrimp for Aggie. "Our destiny!" is just how she'd put it. Since Aggie was born on the beach. "And you love shrimp and I love shrimp," that's what 'rena had said.

But then Lorena did that forgetting thing, that not-talking-much wanting-too-many-hugs thing, so the shrimp had settled into a quiet, way down in the below part of her mind.

161

Mulch's picking up from Chet's shrimp farm chatter, had Chet remembering though. Chet would hardly have put it to words, but he was feeling something like 'Well gosh, fulfilling destinies is nothing to take lightly,' in a manner of speaking ... though Chet wasn't. At Mulch's encouraging though, Chet did see reason to bring to Celeste a general sort of question. 'Was there anything else they needed for making shrimp?'

His intent got lost at dinner though as everyone went gaga over the new "Cod Nuggets 'n Chips."

"Lorena," Delaney caught her arm as Lorena was stepping up to the pass-through for fourths. "What did you put in this batter? The cod nuggets are not only the biggest I've ever seen, they're delicious."

"Oh I can't tell you, sorry Delaney. It's our St. Anne secret recipe."

Regoire sent an apologetic shrug Delaney's direction, but Delaney waved him off with a silly several-syllable gesture meaning to convey how good it was to have Lorena asserting herself.

Clearly Lorena didn't see their exchange. "But you can keep getting taste tests and try to guess. That's all right, right Regoire?" Lorena zoomed on as if he'd responded. "Regoire said Thom found out about fish, that fish are good for growing bodies. Something about the inside functions, that was your word, right Regoire? Of the eaters not the fish." Delaney nodded as if Lorena was making perfect sense. "So We're going to make our cod nuggets and chips dinner twice a month. Maybe more."

"Dessert everyone?"

"Yum, Regoire! I'll be right back, you wait, Aggie."

Lorena looped her arm into the high chair, gave Aggie a squeeze.

While lending Regoire a hand clearing the table, Stuart had a question for Celeste, "Would you like to Skype with Sadie and Richie in a bit?"

"Oh Stuart, I'm afraid I'm done with the computer." She

thought surely Regoire would be pleased.

Chet threw a look Mulch's way.

Regoire was just filling the pass-through with cups of mango sorbet and dainty ginger crisps. "I'll be ready in just a minute, Stuart. I'd like to talk to the kids too."

"Is it all right, Celeste?" Stuart lifted her laptop to the front of her desk while waiting for Lorena to return. "Maybe we could press Restart on this computer business. There's nothing wrong with using it judiciously, especially to keep in touch with loved ones."

Mulch sent a nudging 'See' back to Chet.

Celeste, out-voted, acquiesced. "It would be wonderful to see Sadie and that brother of yours, Bobby." She reached to pat his hand.

Lorena had her head into the sunroom but before Stuart could get out that they were going to Skype, Lorena did that turn-on-her-heel trick with "Oh! I'll be right back. I left my stool in the bathroom."

From Thom to Stuart to Delaney, to Mare to Bobby, Regoire coming out of la cuisine with the tea, to Celeste, not a one of them made eye contact with another. Mare held back her shaking, only just, but Bobby couldn't stop the tears streaming down his cheek. Delaney leaned into, buried her head in Stuart's shoulder in effort to not make a sound. Chet looked uncomfortable but only because he didn't understand.

Mulch patted the boy's leg with a "She'lls be right back. 's sumpin we been workin' on together. 's been dryin'," which didn't do a thing to ensure the hold-back of a snort and a half around the room.

Celeste covered her heart with her hand and Regoire matched the gesture. Though Thom and Reyoire saw Lorena as an adult, in this case they held with Celeste, 'such a vulnerable child.'

And there she came, Aggie banging her high chair tray to Lorena's holding aloft a roughly carved and rudimentarily pegged artisan's stool, just the right height *to pull up to the sunroom table.*

"See," she plunked it down next to Aggie's high chair, "I can feed my pumpkin so much easier from a stool. It's perfect, Mulch," signing him thumbs up which Chet mirrored from across the room. "And all dry now!" as she stroked what might be cosmos that she'd painted on the wooden seat.

Lorena positioned her toes carefully as she slipped onto the stool to help Aggie with dessert. In the cracks where the legs were joined by the rungs Lorena had stuck tufts of baby's breath which in this moment at least, Aggie was unable to harvest.

Aggie fell asleep in Celeste's arms. As they were Skyping, Celeste was stilled in waves of thankfulness. Not a one in the room repeated Lorena's comment to Sadie and Richie, not a one made fun at Lorena's expense. Mulch who thought the whole cyber chatting as much nonsense as smart phones and answering machines, had left, but everyone else took their turns, bantering back and forth like old times.

Sadie innocently asked Lorena how their shrimp tank was coming along.

"Sadie, oh! We haven't got our shrimp yet! Where are our plans, Chet? Mulch, do you know where we put the plans?"

"Mulch went home, 'rennie."

"We'll go get him."

Regoire to Sadie, "And they're off!"

"I'm sorry, Regoire, did I say something wrong?"

"No, no, it'll be good for everyone if we have a new topic ... eh, new project going. The shrimp had somehow lost momentum on their way to St. Anne. We'll keep you posted."

"Celeste, don't worry," hearing, Lorena ducked back in. "Shrimp and chicken go really well together. Don't worry."

"Heavens, I'm not worried, Lorena. Regoire will still make my favorite chicken dishes."

"Don't worry Celeste." Ever Lorena's backer.

"Chet, I'm not at all worried, but thank you."

No, we've not forgotten ... well, actually Delaney did forget during dinner. Surprised herself when she remembered later, going over the evening with Stuart. Mare had noticed but chose to wait. A better time would present itself to bring up the addition to Fix It. Cooling jets wouldn't hurt a thing.

"He said he'd do it."

"Whose said who'd do what, there, Miss Lorena." Mulch tried to slow her down.

"Regoire would make a cream shrimp soup to try out on Aggie. If she likes it, we go ahead. If she doesn't, we'll have shrimp soup for lunch! Next Tuesday, he said."

Lorena was like a kid on a souped up Yamaha, lurching forward trying to stay on for this accelerating ride, 'round and round a track. The mere thought of shrimp swimming in their gardens, in a tub in their garden or however their eventual plans had shrimp swimming ... Lorena couldn't wait. Couldn't wait for Aggie to be able to watch the shrimp. So Lorena fiddled alongside Celeste who was doing her best to find out about shrimp farms. But after only a half hour, Lorena took off. Took Aggie.

Off to the agate mound!

And Chet, even when Celeste had a video clip pulled up, he could not sit still at the computer to watch, so he'd all of a sudden have to go ask something of Mulch and be gone an hour … or more if he got it in mind to check on Lorena and Aggie.

Ultimately Celeste and Mulch found themselves conferring in and out of the sunroom. Mulch would knock, slip his boots off onto the back steps, come in, darned socks leaving wet splotches on the wood floors, glad to 'rest his bones' while Celeste read him the various specifications about raising shrimp.

Mulch and Celeste, sometimes Regoire too as he would linger setting out tea, would get a plan drawn up, adapted from a design online, with a list for Chet to take to the hardware store when Lorena would return from their outing only to throw various changes into the mix. "The tank has to be the right height for Aggie to stand and look into" or "the plastic has to be that kind that won't' hurt Aggie. What is that Chet? Remember, the initials-free kind of plastic. It's Aggie's shrimp farm, Celeste."

Neither Celeste nor Regoire thought it prudent to point out that Lorena's Aggie was not yet two, the whole project better suited for a tenth birthday perhaps. When Celeste suggested Mulch bring up age-appropriateness in the evening while Lorena was over watching his TV, or that Mulch mention to Chet who could then mention to Lorena, during a commercial ... Mulch objected outright.

"Them commercials Chet an' Lorena's favorite part. Awful lotta fun they haves, ratin' 'em 2 to 13 'cording to how much the commercial makes's laugh." And otherwise, Mulch looked at Celeste with his cultivated deadpan followed by 'that is not in my job description' grimace.

So they proceeded in Lorena's unpredictable wake. Backtracking shouldn't have come as a surprise.

"I know the first step," she proclaimed. "I have to take a beginner's class on invertebrates! That's what shrimp are, you know. And I have to start at the beginning for Aggie." Of course in their small coastal town there would be no other class more to the point of small scale shrimp farming, so in that regard Lorena was spot on.

Propulsion fell off in order to accommodate Lorena taking the month-long series at the County Extension. It seemed the most natural thing to Lorena that she leave Aggie with Celeste for her one-night-a-week class.

Lorena's assumption certainly touched Celeste. She'd never admit it though, unless to Thom, as any other ear might mistake her 'wonderment at being wanted' for Celeste thinking herself incapable somehow. Oh yes, in decades past she had been skitterish around little ones. But being with Aggie had been like peeling back the old on a magic slate. Clear page now. Celeste's 'simply being' with Aggie was coming out happy, and good enough.

The first week, unused to separation from Lorena in the evenings, Aggie sucked her thumb so fiercely that Celeste didn't even pause to weigh pros and cons, she just opened her computer and ordered up a pacifier. A mommy approved, zero BPA, most-sustainably manufactured-in-USA pacifier. Speedy delivery, the package arrived before the next class.

The second caring-for-Aggie evening was prefaced by a busy afternoon. So after their good-bye with Lorena, Celeste pulled out the pacifier. That 'pacie' glowed like a godsend, or so Regoire thought too as he rinsed it with water from the kettle. Aggie had been in and out of fussy most of the day.

Way more than Chet's shoulders ever did, things had been hopping around St. Anne. Chet, Mulch, and Lorena as she was able, had been in their usual work mode. Delaney and Bobby had been over at Mare's late afternoon again, encouraging Mare to move forward on her plan to add onto the Fix It. Stuart had stopped by. Mare had decided though that she had a question or two for Thom before she ultimately brought the idea to Celeste.

Once Thom was on his way to the Boulevard, touching in by phone with Regoire, well Regoire would not hear a word other than for the lot of them to come to St. Anne directly after their meet-up.

Celeste was all for the influx, "But dear, how can you manage?" Even if she was the least bit adept in a kitchen, which she was not, Celeste' helping him prep would be out of the question while she was caring for Aggie.

"Celeste, if you don't mind, not a one of our guests will object to my dashing to the market for a good piece of tenderloin. In under an hour I can make you a Bourguignon that you'll think had been cooking all afternoon. And which would you prefer? Pasta or mashed potatoes?"

"You pick, dear. You're the one pulling together a miracle."

That dinner, rather than the previous, turned out the perfect time to discuss the new project. Delaney fed Aggie.

Celeste looked over the plans. When Aggie was full, out came the pacifier and in it went.

Dinner lasted longer than usual as the main lot chattered away, lining up projects for the new workspace. With Celeste's approval and input of little consequence, she was done eating before the others so she had Aggie snuggled on her lap.

When Lorena arrived back in time for dessert, Mare and Bobby, Stuart and Delaney, Chet and Mulch were at the table still just finishing their main course. Thom had stepped into la cuisine to give Regoire a hand setting out dessert. Lorena entered the sunroom reciting some set of invertebrata, rocking her head like a tick tocking clock. When she saw Aggie with the pacifier, Lorena's alarm went off.

"I have never given Aggie a pacifier. Tell her, Chetty. Tell her Mare. I told you, 'no pacifiers' right?"

"Yeah, I've had customers come in with their babies all

muted up, Celeste. On this one, I didn't want to say anything, but I agree with Lorena."

Caught midway between sunroom and la cuisine, only Regoire saw Thom hit palm to forehead.

"What was that for?" Regoire whispered.

"I'll never tell ..." grin spreading. "Well, I might tell you, later.... Much later. Believe me, there are certain people who just never need to know."

"*If you* haven't used ziggurats in a sentence in the last six months, then there's no use you being herewith." Mare couldn't stop the chuckles. What a way to begin a morning, so close to mirth. Day by day she was finding herself in that neighborhood. And when had she ever started a day reading. And for enjoyment. The ziggurats sentence in the book Delaney had left her had latched Mare like a magnet. She might just be able to market ziggurats on the weight of that quote alone, if she could only get clear what a ziggurat was. Or maybe she'd just give them away. To be determined as she hummed "Walking in Sunshine," and remarkably not at all bothered that in her mind's memory Bobby's former girlfriend Bounty filled in the whistling solos.

*Interesting association: vriend (friend)
**Richard Powers "Generosity" p. 6 (perhaps), ziggurats used later p. 81 (for certain)

'There is no way this can go on,' Mare thought. 'I've got work to do.' Still, Mare left her workbench, darn near tiptoed back to her studio to peek inside, read one … then two, three more passages, laughing outright at "What in the name of second chances was [she] thinking."

Chet had taken a long stride out of the kitchen just in time to catch Celeste from coming in.

"Uh Celeste," body hopping as usual, "you don't want to …"

Chet took hold of her shoulders and turned her, but his momentum was so great that he turned her in a 270° circle very nearly facing her back onto the tile.

"Celeste, it's just that …"

Chet repositioned himself between her and the kitchen activity. But as Chet did so his bopping body lost its balance and two feet went right out from under. Thank goodness neither of those were Celeste's.

*Richard Powers "Generosity" again, p. 7

"Oh dear." Celeste tried to reach a hand to pull him up, but Chet wasn't having it.

With palms facing her he kneed his way to the doorjamb then backed into the kitchen, closing her out.

Calling as if over the nonexistent transom, "We have a little problem here, Celeste."

From behind him Celeste could hear Lorena and Aggie, Aggie squealing, Lorena matching with hacky laughs.

"It's not a problem, Celeste!" Lorena corrected Chet. "WOops!"

Now what would have gone down in morning notes if anyone had been doing an observational study on Lorena's little family and gotten a peek where Celeste had not? It's good we're of the mind to give Lorena lots of slack. This is nothing extraordinary ... heavens, it has happened to the best of child care providers and parents in a pinch. Besides, Lorena and Chet would be able retell the story to Aggie. A 'remember when' about how slippery cornmeal play can be when the bin gets accidentally tipped out on the floor and the momma decides in the moment she might as well teach her darling how to skate.

All right then, here we are. Cornmeal slip 'n slide cleaned up, generally speaking. Finally Lorena and Chet were set to get on with the substantially bigger family project. Lorena had studied up shrimp. Celeste had answered the basics for Mulch and by virtue of primary mentorship and a couple of do-it-yourself videos, supposedly the info had passed on to Chet.

"A shrimp farm tank," Chet called it, prophesying more than he could possibly know.

Still and all they did get underway:

- At Lorena's direction, Celeste had ordered the shrimp larvae.
- Chet and Mulch began constructing the Lorena-approved tank. Celeste wheeled out to watch. Since the d-i-y video they were following was in Japanese though,

Lorena and Chet got off track, acting out little by little
"Doozo osaki," alternately puppeting as with a hand sock
then socking it into each other's arms. Neither of which
moved the project along.

• So Mulch had Chet run get Mare who would
understand the cyber feed how-to better than they.

• Upon which Mare took over building while Lorena
instigated more 'saki.'

• Finally, all in readiness, Chet, Lorena and Aggie filled
the tank. The hose kinked, naturally, bursting free all
over them to Aggie's shrieks, at which juncture Mare
ducked out and back to the shop.

• Mulch insisted that 'the kids' replay the youtube video
with Celeste interpreting as best she could to review how
the shrimp larvae be inserted. Even if the best video
available wasn't in a language other than English, for
Chet and Lorena to track a youtube video was like
rehearsing for a play, facing backwards. Or as if the
reel was running backwards because by the time they
got to the end, they weren't prepared to pick up back at

the beginning ... as they were already at the end. Chets and Lorenas need lists one two three.

- Over-ready, Aggie took over, dumping the shrimp in herself, a good half landing on her own feet, the unspotted strays gladdening the chickens in their late afternoon scratch.

"But how much? In English!"

Stuart had come by to check out the inception. "I don't know, Lorena," with his indulgent smile. "I'm not sure if bonking the salinometer on the fence post is going to get it to read any better."

Which set off her "Regoire! We need more salt!"

The topic from then on, chicken coop to la cuisine, back out around the garden: How are those shrimp doing?

Lorena to Regoire, "Did you know shrimp jump?"

Mulch to Chet, "Yous got to find a better way to tie that net down."

182

"Celeste! Something tried to get in the tank. The net is all ..." Lorena's hands went every which way.

"And the shrimp? Are they all there?"

"Aggie's shrimp won't stay still, so we couldn't count them yesterday. We can't count to know if they're the same today. They look the same."

"Well good. Whatever it was most likely got scared off before breakfast."

"What was it?"

"Raccoon maybe. Or fox."

"Chet!" Pivoting out the garden door, "We might have a fox in the lane!"

"If we did," Celeste to Aggie, "we don't now."

And after Celeste answered the phone, "Aggie, it looks like you're going to get to see your Sadie again." Calling to la cuisine, "Regoire did you hear? Sadie and Richie have a break coming up. I said yes of course they can stay in the cottage."

So there we have it, looks like everyone may be gathering again as we head into St. Anne's final Book Four. For now we have a shrimp fiasco ... uh ... farm to wrap.

Picture Aggie one day, packing her stuffed seal about in the garden, draped over her shoulder, sticking out of her pocket, hiding under her hat, the seal you may remember Chet bought her at birth. That night when putting Aggie to bed, Chet had made silly about how seals and shrimp, both, swim in the sea, demonstrating as only Chet would.

Next day sure enough Mare got roped into building a little stand so Aggie's seal could keep watch on the shrimp. A stuffed seal, after all, needed an important job, now that Aggie, or more accurately Lorena had it in her head ... and being stuffed, her seal mustn't do what Chet ... Which is exactly how Lorena entangled Mare into service, first-thing-first.

That afternoon Stuart remarked that the seal's perch looked like a crow's nest, but Lorena squelched that too as overcomplicated for explaining out loud. Mulch didn't help any, inserting "perch ar fish. Don' be fergettin' tha'." Easy to imagine Aggie's mimicking Lorena's sigh. Still, Lorena recorded every detail, how not all crows' nests are for feathereds and not all perches come with fins. And, though she was writing all this out on a 'New Notes to My Daughter' page which she tucked in with her papers on dogs and baselines, Lorena kept it to herself for the time being that ... seals do eat shrimp. As my, Lora's, proxy Celeste could certainly, though silently enough, affirm Lorena's closing words: "Troublesome. Parenting. Can be."

And oh how those shrimp did grow, all the way to edible size. In la cuisine Regoire had his largest stock pot with water on its way to a boil. While from the garden Mulch handled the net, harvesting into Momma, Poppa and baby Aggie's bowls.

Then there was … the long … walk … from the garden, in through the sunroom, and on in to Regoire. Lorena first, followed by her ducky darlin', with Chet whose shoulders had not a bounce in them bringing up the tail, each a caricature of Droop. Yes of course the salt water in Aggie's baby bowl slosh sloshed over her tummy drip drip dripping, tickling her knees. But she had nary a giggle in her. The light shone in through the tri-cornered skylights, execution style, as they passed through the sunroom. By then Lorena had slowed, and for once it wasn't Aggie tugging on her. Aggie padded on, her momma reluctantly stepping in behind. Aggie's pace crumpled too though. She started to whimper, circling her fingers in the bowl she was carrying, one shrimp kicking its little feet.

Unbeknownst to the others, Aggie had a pinch in her stocking, the pointiest of pebbles poking sideways between two toes. As Aggie turned, raising her little face to her momma, a single tear splashed into Aggie's bowl. Lorena saw, assumed that her daughter too was empathizing

186

sorely with the shrimp. The procession came to a confused ka-wumple. Lorena started to bawl. Aggie cried because her momma was crying. Chet tried to comfort both his girls while balancing his poppa size bowl. Spill. Tears. Fits, Lorena's.

Celeste entered from the hallway, but immediately she side-stepped into la cuisine.

"Regoire can we turn this arou...?" but she was stopped mid-sentence by the smell ~ picture wavy lines heading to Celeste's nose ~ as Regoire moved to open the oven. She knew before she could see. Without a word she identified Regoire's glorious hazelnut pie. And two of them! Regoire merely winked ...

"How quickly can you come, can we get on with this? Our little family is ready for a wild release, don't you think."

"Oh it sounds that way. It definitely sounds like a wild release in the making. I'll call Mare."

"Regoire, do you mind if I do?"

"Do it, of course."

"And Stuart and Delaney."

As Celeste was dialing, Regoire rang up Thom on his own cell. "Can you tell, my man, when is high tide?"

It took Thom half a second.

"Perfect. Hold on, Sweets."

To Celeste, "High tide's at 3:21. Get everybody who can down to the agate mound."

Thom into Regoire's phone. "I heard. I can call Bobby. What have you and Celeste cooked up?"

Regoire spoke in abbreviated code, the kind only couples can understand. "I'll see you then."

Bobby picked right up, "I'll bring clam shovels. It won't take anything for us to dig a nice little trench to flush the shrimp through."

"Great idea ... only Bobby, we might want to stay clear of the word 'flush,' eh?"

"Right. Right!"

Ready to spring the wild release idea on their dears, Celeste had her hand on the door to the sunroom when Regoire with a flourish opened his other oven and wafted his mitt in Celeste's direction. Celeste couldn't have loved him more.

"How did you know, Regoire?"

"I had a feeling, that's all. Now, I'd better go help Mulch get those shrimp back into their tank. What do you think?"

"I think you are a wizard of the finest order. And what is it you've concocted for our main course, if not shrimp?"

"Blanquette de poulet. I've got enough to cover the lot of us."

Muffled, "Funny, Regoire."

Now you might or might not recognize the French word for chicken. Considering domains, it's not surprising that Regoire would already be a long stride ahead. What if Lorena at some point extended her dreadful recognition of wiggly critters, in this case so alarmingly shrimp-sized, on to larger even more obvious animals that regularly head through la cuisine, and onto their sunroom table. If an invertebrate could set Lorena off so, pulling the plug on creamed shrimp soup, heaven forbid she pass that revelation on to Aggie. Regoire would do whatever it took to obviate culinary mutiny at St. Anne.

Yes, you're following, from that day forward any dish that featured a meat, especially chicken … the cousins of which pecked freely along St. Anne's own borders … any such dish that Regoire placed on the pass-through would be announced in French, whether of French acclaim or not. Heavens, Celeste was too old and the both of them way too set to switch. In cahoots, Mulch saw to it that there were plenty of new and enticing treats to be had out of their own garden, if and when further distraction be's needed.

And though, even tended things could get jumbled, or one might say 'more lively' as time went on, the addition at Fix It did get completed, eventually allowing for anyone at St. Anne to have a hand in whatever project popped up, or in some cases hands in dubious dismantling.

Yes, Lora here too, looking forward to meeting up with you one more time

through the lane ...